THE
Asheville
CHRISTMAS
CABIN

❯❯ CAROLINA CHRISTMAS * BOOK ONE ❮❮

HOPE HOLLOWAY
AND
CECELIA SCOTT

Hope Holloway and Cecelia Scott

Carolina Christmas Book 1

The Asheville Christmas Cabin

Cover design by Kim Killion, The Killion Group

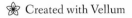 Created with Vellum

A Personal Note from the Authors

Welcome to the mountains of Asheville, North Carolina, the backdrop for our first collaborative writing endeavor. We hope you love the sisters, the story, and the setting of this holiday trilogy as much as we do. This concept was born during a week-long cabin vacation with our husbands, while we watched the sun rise over the Blue Ridge Mountains. Enchanted with Asheville and the surrounding area—where Cece lived a few years ago—we started brainstorming the story of three sisters who returned to the mountains for a life-changing holiday. The idea got ahold of us and soon we were sketching out characters, plots, and a system for co-writing that has worked wonderfully. We like to think of this trilogy as a Christmas gift to our readers who've been loyal and enthusiastic since we started writing. We hope you are enchanted, delighted, and warmed by this Carolina Christmas.

With love and joy,
Hope & Cece

This trilogy is dedicated with love to our angel in heaven, sweet Sarah.
We miss you every day.

The Carolina Christmas Trilogy

The Asheville Christmas Cabin – book 1
The Asheville Christmas Gift – book 2
The Asheville Christmas Wedding – book 3

Prologue

Elizabeth

A WINTER HUSH fell over the cabin as Elizabeth Whitaker walked through the two-story great room, warmed by the crackling fire and the waning daylight that poured over the hardwood floors. After sixty-three Thanksgiving Days in her lifetime, she knew the sun was setting on one of the best she'd ever celebrated. But earlier that day, as she'd bowed her head in gratitude and awe, she'd had a stark realization.

It was time to tell the girls.

"But how?" she asked the empty room.

Not exactly empty, though, was it? Her dearly departed sister, gone twenty-five years, had left her spirit imbued in every inch of this great mountain cabin outside of Asheville, North Carolina. From the gabled roof to the wide wooden deck and all through the knotty pine walls inside, the memory of Jacqueline Whitaker Chambers remained alive in this home. And because of that, Elizabeth had stayed away for all but the last of those twenty-five years.

But now, there'd been a change. A big change. And

that meant it was time to bring Jackie's daughters back to Asheville.

As much as Elizabeth longed to pull out a pen and paper and write an old-fashioned letter to her three nieces, she knew that would take too long and a piece of mail could get lost in their busy lives. Plus, they were all together for the Thanksgiving holiday, so an email would be best, instant, and give them a chance to mull over her invitation together.

To make sure they understood the weight of what she was asking, she decided to draft her note on digital stationery, complete with holiday decorations and Christmas cuteness, like those annoying annual letters people send every year. That would keep it light, and get her message across when she sent it as an image to their email boxes. Anyone else might not understand, but those girls certainly would.

At the dining table, she opened her laptop and entered three names, in birth order. Eve Gallagher, Angie Messina, and Noelle Chambers.

She stared at the names, picturing each of the sisters who were like daughters to her, a woman who'd never had children of her own. The Chambers triplets— although two were married and had different last names now—were all turning forty next month and she'd adored them from the day they'd been born.

That memorable day had been unlike any other Christmas, with her sister Jackie going into labor early on December twenty-fourth. Just before midnight, the first baby was born and that baby girl was, of course, named Eve.

Today, Eve Chambers Gallagher was sweet and gentle, with pale blond hair and kind blue eyes and a steely determination to achieve control and perfection in her world. The thought made Elizabeth smile, since control and perfection were next to impossible for Eve, who had three active, busy young boys.

But Eve was an exceptional mother to those kids, a devoted wife, and a woman in love with the very idea of love, as was evident by her happy marriage. Of her three nieces, Elizabeth knew Eve would be the most receptive to this note.

Angie might be a little bewildered, but she'd come around. Officially the second baby born, although after the clock had struck midnight on Christmas, Angel blessed them all with her wit and wisdom and natural warmth. She became known as Angie quite quickly and with her curly, butterscotch blond hair and green eyes that lit with curiosity and charisma, she was somehow the glue that held those three together.

But Angie Messina was struggling right now. Not that she'd come right out and admitted that. She didn't have to. Elizabeth guessed that due to Angie's ever-absent husband and recently-turned-sullen teenaged daughter, things were not copacetic in California. Maybe this letter could help change that.

And last was Noelle Chambers, the brunette beauty with impossibly dark eyes that reflected ambition and the will to be the best at whatever she did. When Elizabeth had stepped in as a substitute parent after theirs had been tragically killed, Noelle had clung the tightest. As the years went by, Noelle had done everything she could to emulate Elizabeth.

Without trying, Elizabeth had become Noelle's motivator and mentor, helping to shape the unattached career woman with big goals and fierce independence. Because of that, Elizabeth was certain Noelle would be the one most deeply affected by—and opposed to—change.

And, whoa, this was a change.

With a deep, steadying breath, she tapped the keys and started the letter the way she always addressed these three...

My dearest darlings...

She paused, looking through the floor-to-ceiling glass of the sunroom, studying the dusky grays and silver tones of the Blue Ridge Mountains rolling off to infinity. Oh, these hills held memories. Some beautiful and happy, some dark and sad.

Would the girls come back? Would they understand? Would they bring their families, their work, their good, good hearts? Could a Christmas at the Asheville cabin help heal them the way a year here had changed Elizabeth?

Eve, Angie, and Noelle all needed her in different ways, but they didn't know that yet.

As she finished the note, keeping it light, fun, and purposefully vague, she said a quick prayer and hit Send.

Now, she'd just have to wait and see how her nieces responded.

Chapter One

Noelle

"ANOTHER DAY OFF? Two in a row? What is this madness of which you speak?" Noelle Chambers gave a playful laugh but she wasn't really kidding. "Other than today, I honestly don't think I've taken a day off in a year and now you guys want me to take two?"

"Oh, honey. That's sad." Her sister, Eve, offered a pitying look as she came out to the chilly air of her patio carrying three cups of Irish coffee on a rustic wood tray. All the glass mugs were topped with whipped cream and the ideal amount of chocolate shavings, of course. From the vineyard lights to the elegant furnishings, Eve's Charlotte, North Carolina backyard proved that the woman would settle for nothing less than perfection.

"Sad, but true," Noelle acknowledged, taking the cup Eve offered. "I once worked from the bathroom floor when I had food poisoning. Not lying."

Noelle took a deep inhale of the heady aroma of coffee and whiskey, instantly awash in memories of many nights spent like this with her two sisters and their favorite decadent beverage. "This better not be decaf,

Eve. I need some kick to stay up and go through emails for a few hours. I've lost this entire day."

Next to Noelle on the loveseat, Angie rolled her eyes and swirled her cup. "This entire day? It was *Thanksgiving*, for heaven's sake. And tomorrow is a holiday extension, so even the Sotheby's Director of Luxury Art Management can take the day off."

Noelle grinned. "Soon to be *Senior* Director, I hope. I'll never get my dream job in London if I don't get this promotion."

"You'll get it," Eve said confidently. "And then you'll get the next one, in London, not that I'm happy about you being that far away."

"Please, it's all I want in the world, but it'll be at least a year, assuming I get this next promotion. You know I pre-celebrated and splurged on a Louis Vuitton limited edition Neverfull bag, so that new title better be mine."

"Here's what you can do with your bag." Angie leaned in, her teasing smile making her green eyes dance. "Put your laptop in it and zip it closed. You are *not* working tonight or tomorrow. I had to move heaven and Earth—also known as leaving my husband and daughter in California over the Thanksgiving holiday—in order to make this triplets reunion happen. Our time together is too rare to spend one second working."

Noelle couldn't argue that, she thought as she tasted the sweet whipped cream and looked from one sister to the other, giving in to the peace that came from being with these two amazing women.

Angie was right. These days were too precious for the sisters not to soak up every second.

"Fine," she agreed. "Until Saturday, when I head back to New York, I will not so much as open my laptop or pick up my phone, which I left in the kitchen." She looked pointedly at the two phones on the table in front of them. "Can't say the same for you two."

"Touché," Angie conceded. "But I have a sixteen-year-old daughter across the country, so an emergency meltdown is always a possibility."

"And I have three sons playing video games in the den upstairs," Eve chimed in. "Any minute one of them—you know which one—could decide to come down using only the banister under his backside. Out of deference to my special time with you two, I asked the oldest to text me if the Wild Thing gets out of control."

They all nodded, having seen the "out of control" happen right after six-year-old Sawyer's second slice of pumpkin pie hit bottom.

"He's a doll," Angie said. "They all are. And this house?" She made a sweeping gesture to encompass the red brick Georgian that Eve and her husband had built and decorated like a showplace. The house was perched on a rise in the suburbs of Charlotte, with a commanding view of hills and a glistening lake in the distance. "I love the lot you picked out here, too."

"Thanks. To be honest, it's more than I want or need, but David earned it. He calls it The House That Brain Surgery Built." Eve grabbed two fuzzy throws from the basket next to her, tossing one to her sisters and tucking herself under another. "The only problem is the brain surgeon works so hard, he's hardly ever in the house to enjoy it. Case in point: tonight."

"That was an emergency," Angie said.

"David's *life* is an emergency," Eve countered. "But it was nice to have him for the turkey and all, if not the pie. And, yes, we love the house. It's spacious and wonderful and since I homeschool three boys, we need that."

"It kind of reminds me of Mom and Dad's house in Raleigh," Noelle mused. "Obviously, that place was smaller, but it has that same homey vibe that Mom always created."

Eve responded with a huge smile. "That's such a compliment, Noelle. I definitely channeled our wonderful mom when I decorated. Did Jackie Chambers ever meet a winged-back chair she didn't re-cover in chintz and love?"

They laughed at the memory, while Noelle nestled closer to Angie, the warmth of the blanket, the whiskey-flavored coffee, and the well-placed heat lamps settling over her. Or maybe it was the decision to take tomorrow off to be with her sisters. That felt good, too.

She dropped her head on Angie's shoulder with a happy sigh. "Is your place cozy in California, Ange? I can't believe you've lived there four years and I haven't been out yet." She grunted. "I'm the worst."

"You're busy selling—and buying—luxury art and getting fat promotions," Angie said, letting her off the hook. "And nothing's cozy in Menlo Park, least of all the ultramodern Messina home that Craig insisted we buy.

The view's nice, but the floors are made of literal concrete without benefit of carpet or a piece of hardwood. It's like living in a Home Depot, only not as many hot construction guys running around."

"Angie." Eve sat forward, a frown pulling. "That's gotta be the third less-than-wonderful comment you've made about living out there. Are you not happy?"

She shrugged, forcing Noelle to lift her head. "I'm happy enough."

"What does that mean?" Noelle asked, hearing the unmistakable note of defeat in her sister's voice.

"It means life is fine. My husband is...distracted and caught up in the Silicon Valley craziness and the schedule of a high-tech marketing guru. My daughter is a wildly dramatic, totally judgmental, utterly self-involved sixteen-year-old. But aren't they all?"

"We weren't," Eve said softly.

At her tone, the three women shared a look, knowing exactly what they were around that age. Broken, orphaned, and forever changed by a semi-truck that crossed the median and crashed head-on into their parents' car three days after the Christmas when they turned fifteen.

Nothing was really ever the same after that dark day twenty-five years ago, with the possible exception of the relationship between the three sisters. They'd only grown closer in the ensuing years. Time and geography and jobs and families had spread them out to three states and separate lives, but they remained as connected today as they'd once been in their mother's womb.

"Enough about me," Angie said with a brisk change of subject. "Eve's the one with a crazy life."

"Seriously," Noelle agreed, knowing that no matter how hectic her own career-focused life got, her schedule wasn't quite the juggling job that Eve's was. "Three boys under eleven. I do not know how you do it."

"Most days, neither do I," Eve said with a self-deprecating laugh. "Homeschooling can get wild—so many projects! And, of course, there isn't a sport they don't love, an activity they don't excel in, or a friend they don't have. Oh, did I mention my youngest is...a climber?"

"Tie the kid down and call it a day," Angie joked.

Eve laughed. "Don't think I haven't considered it. But, honestly, I can't complain. I have a wonderful, overwhelming, sometimes breathlessly hectic life. And Christmas looms, the nemesis of every obsessive mother."

"Like ours." Noelle closed her eyes, the talk of their late mother touching that bittersweet place in her heart. "She used to start in early November, remember? All the gifts and ridiculous ribbons."

"The bigger the ribbon, the smaller the gift," Angie quipped. "She insisted the Asheville cabin get decked out with six billion lights, a tree that filled the two-story living room, and if it didn't snow, she made Dad rent a snow machine and give us a white Christmas. Now, that woman was the original overachiever."

Noelle smiled, but had to defend their Christmas-crazy mom. "She had to go overboard because it is a very big day for the Chambers triplets. I think she felt a little guilty it was Christmas *and* our birthday."

"Your birthday," Eve corrected, picking up her Irish coffee. "I was born at 11:58 on Christmas Eve. You two slackers didn't show for ten more minutes."

The ding of a phone notification interrupted the conversation and had Eve and Angie both reaching for their phones.

"Uh-oh," Noelle teased, happy to not have hers in hand for once. "Is it Sawyer flying down the stairs or is there a teenage breakdown out in California?"

"It's..." Eve tapped the phone. "An email from..." She clicked again, quiet as she read, then looked up at Angie. "Did you get this, too?"

Angie was reading, her jaw slack. "Is this a joke?"

"What?" Noelle demanded, leaning forward to see Angie's phone.

"Go get your phone and see if you got an email from Aunt Elizabeth," Angie said. "And...if you believe it."

"Aunt Elizabeth!" Noelle rose at the mention of the only woman she loved as much as these two. "A Happy Thanksgiving note? Where is she, anyway? Paris? Dubai? To be honest, I haven't heard from her in a good long while."

And that, Noelle realized as she walked into the house, was odd. Since their parents died, Elizabeth Whitaker had been a constant in their lives. Their eccentric and sophisticated aunt had picked up the pieces of three devastated girls that horrible holiday week, then she took over the job of their parents.

Like a second mother, Aunt Elizabeth had moved her

jet-setting life to Raleigh and done her level best to help them navigate tragedy and the rest of high school.

And, as the years passed, Elizabeth continued to be a mother to them all, and a real inspiration to Noelle.

It was Aunt Elizabeth who'd taught Noelle everything about independence and success. So much so that Noelle had taken art history and business in college, then followed her aunt's footsteps into a career as a luxury art dealer.

Aunt Elizabeth, who'd moved back to her pied-à-terre in New York after the sisters had gone to college, never missed a milestone in Noelle's career, or in any of their lives. She'd popped the champagne when Noelle had gotten her entry-level job at Sotheby's and continued to celebrate every promotion Noelle achieved for the next ten years.

"Let me guess," Noelle called to them while she scanned the kitchen for her bag. "She's trying to rope us into a Christmas trip."

Their aunt's holiday excursions had started the year after Jackie and Jim Chambers had been killed. They hadn't gone to Asheville that summer, of course, and the following fall, Aunt Elizabeth announced that they never would go back to the cabin again, not even for Christmas.

After fifteen years of Decembers at the sprawling mountain home that had been in their mother's family for generations, tradition changed.

Their aunt dubbed the holiday "Birthmas" and gathered up the girls for what became an annual trip, always somewhere glamorous, far away, and unforgettable. She said she didn't want the sisters to be sad by going to the cabin. But as they got older, they realized it was their aunt who couldn't bear the family Christmases at the magical log manor without her own dear sister.

Aunt Elizabeth and their mother had been as close as Noelle, Angie, and Eve were. Once, after a few of those champagne toasts, Aunt Elizabeth had confessed that she would never again step foot in the Asheville home that had been in her family for generations.

She kept it for rentals, had a property manager handle repairs, but none of them had ever gone back to the place where they'd had the best summers and the most amazing Christmases.

And that was sad, but understandable. They'd been at the cabin the night a police officer knocked on the door, interrupting a rousing game of Scrabble they had been playing with Aunt Elizabeth while Mom and Dad were on a date night.

The Asheville cabin held both beautiful and brutal memories, which Aunt Elizabeth worked to wipe away with her wonderful trips.

Truth be told, Noelle thought as she finally dug out her phone, she certainly wouldn't hate a Christmas somewhere far away with her sophisticated and luxury-loving aunt.

Holidays alone were...not fun. Busy as all get-out at work, but the nights could be lonely no matter how many parties she attended.

"Noelle," Eve called from the back patio. "Did you see it?"

"Coming." She returned to the patio without even looking at the email, still feeling kind of giddy about whatever exciting trip her aunt was proposing. "I know you two can't drop everything, and really, I shouldn't either, but..."

"Read it," Eve said, her voice unnaturally flat.

Noelle frowned, her stomach dropping with worry. "Is she okay?"

"That remains to be seen," Angie said. "Read it and tell us what you think."

Bracing herself for bad news, Noelle clicked on the newest item in her inbox. She gave it a second to load, then recoiled in surprise at the colors and images and all the...was that a *sleigh* along the top border?

"Is she doing a holiday letter to the masses now?" Noelle asked.

"Just read it," Eve and Angie said in perfect unison.

"I can't get past the reindeer. Is she serious?"

"I'll read it," Angie said, picking up her phone, clearing her throat to mimic Aunt Elizabeth's clipped and refined tone. "'My dearest darlings! I miss you three angels so much! I know I've been quiet lately, but my life has taken a surprising turn. I want to share it with you in person, and I want to do it in style. I am requesting— some might say insisting—that we all spend the entire month of December at the Asheville cabin and celebrate the holiday together.'"

"What?" Noelle choked as she read along. "A year ago, she said she was considering selling the place. Now she wants to spend a *month* there?"

Eve nodded. "Read the last line."

Angie did the honors again. "'You may, of course, bring your families. Also, your computers—there's Wi-Fi now—which means I will accept no excuses. Doors open on December first, there's plenty of room, and all the decorations are here in the attic. I need your assistance in decking the halls, fa-la-la and ho ho ho! Sending you oodles of love, Aunt E.'"

For a good long moment, none of them spoke as it all sank in.

"Wow," Eve finally whispered. "Did aliens abduct our Christmas-hating, world-traveling, dry martini-sipping aunt? I mean..." She lifted up her phone, pointing to the email. "Was that a gingerbread cookie in her signoff? Who *is* she?"

"I'm actually speechless," Angie said on a wry laugh. "I didn't even think she went to the cabin anymore! And she wants us all to come for an entire month?"

"Wait. Wait. *Wait.*" Noelle held out her hand. "First of all, she says her life 'has taken a surprising turn.' Do you think she's sick?"

"She certainly doesn't sound unhappy."

"Just crazy," Angie cracked.

"And she also says she wants us 'here'—so she's there now, at the cabin." Noelle looked from one sister to the other. "Three hours away in the Blue Ridge Mountains? How is this possible?"

"Anything's possible with that woman," Angie said. "She's the most unpredictable person in the family."

"Not when it comes to Christmas," Noelle said. "She

hates the holiday without her sister. She hates the memories, the anniversary on the twenty-eighth, and has never wanted anything but to focus on our birthdays, not Christmas."

Eve leaned back and exhaled slowly. "I don't know what's up with her," she said. "But I, for one, have ached to go back to that cabin."

"Well, you can go," Angie said. "It's a three-hour drive from here. I can't skip Thanksgiving *and* Christmas with my family."

"She said to bring them," Eve countered. "There's plenty of room in that place."

"I don't know," Noelle said, still processing this bizarre invitation. "Maybe it's a joke? She does have a weird sense of humor."

"She doesn't joke about Christmas or that cabin," Eve replied. "It has so many memories, good and bad. There has to be a great reason for asking us to go there."

Eve had a point. Their aunt not only didn't joke about it, she barely mentioned the holiday. It was their birthday, first and foremost, and an excuse to go somewhere amazing. Somewhere that *wasn't* the Asheville cabin.

"I'm going," Eve announced. "Nothing can stop me. I've wanted to take the boys there for years, but whenever I have asked Aunt Elizabeth, she says it's rented."

"Well, I don't know." Angie made a face, glancing off into the darkness, her shoulders sinking. "My husband and daughter coming with me to the middle of nowhere in the mountains for the entire holiday season? The chances of that happening are about as likely as Aunt Elizabeth adopting a pet pig."

Noelle snorted. "Don't give that woman any ideas. Evidently nothing is off the table."

Eve's shoulder-length blond hair swayed as she looked back and forth between the two other women. "We can't just say no to her. She certainly never said no to us. We owe her this much."

Noelle shut her eyes. "We owe her everything," she agreed, then looked down at her phone. "But why this? Why the cabin? And why Christmas?"

Angie nodded. "It's totally weird. Maybe a little scary. I admit, I'm curious. I suppose I could run it by Craig and see if we can swing part of the month."

Noelle sipped lukewarm Irish coffee as reality set in. "A *month*? I don't take a day off, as I mentioned."

"Well, you need to," Eve replied. "And maybe Aunt Elizabeth knows that. Just like she knows Angie might need a change of scenery, and that I might need...a break from life."

"I doubt my husband and daughter will be on board, but...I'll do my best." Angie smiled from one to the other. "I want to do this with you guys. This seems special and important. It feels different, I can't deny that."

Noelle fully agreed with that. This wildly out of character invitation had to mean something, didn't it?

"I'm worried about her," she confessed. "It's not like Aunt Elizabeth to be out of touch, but she's traveling and busy so I haven't heard much from her lately. What about you guys?"

"Just once in a while," Angie said. "You, Eve?"

"I texted her that you two would be here for Thanksgiving a while back, and she just wrote back that it sounded wonderful, but didn't ask to join us," Eve said, sighing as if she made a decision. "I don't know if David can be there the whole time, but I'll be there with the boys. You two?"

"Maybe," Angie said. "It sure sounds better than concrete floors and painfully sunny days in Menlo Park. I'll do my best."

They looked at Noelle, who felt an inexplicable churning. Part of her wanted to run to Aunt Elizabeth, no matter what her reason. Part of her wanted to...meet her deadlines, sell her art, get that promotion, and then next Christmas, she might be headed to London. But another part of her really wanted to be with her sisters and not alone in New York. She just assumed she would because her biggest client was having an auction of his world-class collection in December.

"I don't know," she said, feeling the insistent gazes of both her sisters. Two of the three people in the world she loved the most—the other being Aunt Elizabeth—stared at her with hope and anticipation in their eyes.

"Come on," Eve urged. "You love that mountain. You always called it your happy place when we were packing up for a trip."

Noelle gave her a wistful smile. "It was happy," she said. "I loved waking up in that upstairs back room and seeing a deer in the yard."

"And taking Rascal for walks in the woods," Eve

added, making them all smile when they thought of the boxer they loved so much. "Remember the creek? And how we'd fish with Dad?"

"Oh, I remember the creek," Noelle said, another smile pulling.

"You remember kissing Jace Fleming outside that dilapidated shack the day after Christmas?" Angie teased her.

"What?" Noelle shrieked. "How do you know that?"

"We were spying," Eve said on a laugh, reaching out her hand to give Angie a high-five. "How did we keep that from her for all these years?"

"We were going to tell Mom but Aunt Elizabeth talked us out of it," Angie said. "Then, you know, other things happened that week."

Noelle nodded and let out a sigh. "Jace was a cutie and I never said goodbye. We just left after... Well, we just left. We never called each other or talked again."

"Look," Eve said, leaning forward. "There are way more good memories at that cabin than bad. I say we all go. Our aunt needs us and that should be the only thing that matters."

"And let's not forget the elephant in the room," Angie added. "It *will* be our fortieth birthday."

Noelle sucked in a breath as she realized that...and the fact that she *couldn't* say no. Not to them, not to Aunt Elizabeth. She had a laptop and the cabin had Wi-Fi and her work could technically be done from anywhere as long as someone from Sotheby's covered for her at the auction. She'd share her commission and her boss would understand. Family was that important.

"Okay. I'll make it work," she said.

"Yes!" Eve jumped up and pulled them both along with her. "Christmas *and* birthdays at the Asheville cabin!"

Eve grabbed her nearly empty mug off the table and raised it in a toast, beaming as the moonlight glinted off her glowing skin and pretty eyes. "Cheers to our birthdays, to Christmas, to the cabin, and to our crazy aunt. May we make some much-needed new and happy memories this December."

Noelle and Angie lifted their mugs and tapped them all together in a toast to the unexpected.

As they hugged, Noelle had one more thought. Had she signed that weird note, "Aunt E"? The woman never called herself anything but "Elizabeth"—ever.

Yeah, she had to go. Something was definitely up.

Chapter Two

Angie

"DID YOU SAY A MONTH?" Craig nearly spit the question, a lock of black hair tumbling over his brow as he recoiled in shock. "Like the whole of December? In... where is this place again? Asheville?"

Angie wasn't surprised by her husband's reaction, but in the few days between making the decision with her sisters and flying back to California, she'd foolishly hoped he'd love the idea. Maybe she should have waited a day instead of making the announcement mere minutes after she arrived home.

She'd harbored hope because Craig could be unpredictable, which was once one of the things she loved most about him.

"That is patently the stupidest thing I've ever heard, Angie."

And he could be nasty, which was not on the loveable list.

"So, no, we're not going," he added, reminding her that stubborn was yet another one of those traits she couldn't stand.

That list was growing, no matter how hard she tried to make this less-than-perfect marriage work.

"It's a month, yes, but it's a month when a lot of people take personal time to be with family." She leaned against the endless gray island, trying not to compare this modern glass and concrete box with Eve's inviting country kitchen. "I, for one, would like to be with my family, and we were invited by my Aunt Elizabeth."

Turning from the bar where he'd just poured a scotch on the rocks—without so much as offering her a glass of water—he shrugged. "Now, if your Aunt Lizzie wants to fly us all to Paris or London, we might talk."

Irritation scampered up her spine. "First of all, anyone who calls her anything except *Elizabeth* doesn't live to tell the tale. Second, the invitation is specific and clear: the cabin in Asheville for Christmas."

He took a deep drink, eyeing her over the rim. "I'm pretty sure this is the aunt who took you and your sisters to Bora Bora or Hawaii or Japan on Christmas specifically to *avoid* the holiday and that very cabin. You sure she's not messing with you?"

Angie shrugged. "She said she has something to share, and I really think it's important that we go."

"We?" Craig narrowed his eyes in a way that looked so mean and vicious she struggled to recognize him as the man who'd wiped a tear as he waited at the end of the aisle on their wedding day. This was...someone else.

Ever since he took this job four years ago, he'd changed. It was slow and insidious at first, the impact of the Silicon Valley life on a man who'd been living in

Atlanta for many years. But recently, the changes seemed to intensify. The past year, she sometimes didn't know who he was. He drank more, he snapped constantly, and he found endless excuses to be anywhere but home.

Could that be fixed? Good heavens, she hoped so. But doubts she hated to admit she had continued to creep into every thought she had about him.

"Yes, *we*," she said softly. "A trip like this might do us a world of good, Craig. We could hike and make fires and, oh, if it snows—"

"I am not going to Christmas Camp, Angie." He made the pronouncement with nothing but vitriol in his voice. Did he hate her that much?

"I know it sounds crazy, Craig, but—"

"Sounds crazy? It sounds like you have absolutely no sense of anything. I'm the Vice-President of Marketing at Atlas Technologies." He dragged out the title like he was announcing his royal blood.

Angie inhaled a shuddering breath. "I'm well aware of what you do, Craig. Noelle has a really important and demanding job, too, and she's going to come and work remotely. Maybe you could consider doing something like that."

Craig turned away, and Angie felt that now familiar... drain. Somehow, his anger and distance and ice-cold shoulder sucked the spark out of her, along with her enthusiasm and joy.

On a normal day-to-day basis, she'd become accustomed to the feeling of always toning herself down, replacing any vibrance with a soft, gentle, agreeable chill that didn't set him off.

But right now? After being immersed in love and laughter and the ability to be her realest self with her sisters, it deeply hurt to have to hide her personality from her own husband.

Thanksgiving in Charlotte felt like a hazy fever dream. Now, she was here, in this gargantuan glass house, feeling like she'd left her spirit and sparkle three thousand miles away.

"Honestly, Angie, the fact that you would even ask me to work remotely from some cabin out in the redneck boonies is actually kind of offensive." He downed the drink and held up a hand. "We're done here."

Oh, yes, my friend, we are done.

She swallowed against a lump in her throat, a little sorry she hadn't been more honest with Eve and Noelle. Maybe they could have advised her on how to save this faltering marriage. She simply hadn't wanted to admit failure, not to happily-married Eve or wildly successful and independent Noelle.

She couldn't simply...call it quits, could she?

"Wait," she said, reaching out to snag Craig's arm as he headed out. "Please. I've missed you."

He hesitated, and gave a nod. "Yeah, I missed you, too."

Sliding her hand down his arm to take his hand, she lifted it to her heart. "I'm worried about us," she whispered.

He searched her face, silent, even though he looked

like he had a lot to say.

"Can we please just consider finding a way to make this work?" she asked.

Craig stayed frozen, every muscle still. He didn't melt at her touch the way he used to. "By this do you mean... this?" He lifted their joined hands, then freed his. "Or some interminable trip to nowhere with a bunch of people I don't even like?"

"Craig, please."

"Sorry, I know it's your family," he said quickly, as if even he realized how low that blow was. "But look, I have the sales conference in Cancun the second week in December—"

"You do?" She'd gone with him the last time the annual meeting had been in Mexico. He'd waited until now to tell her?

"No spouses this year," he shot back. "Budget cuts."

"Oh, okay." Her heart sank, and she tried to think of when Atlas cut anything, least of all their grand trip to shower the sales force with love. "But you could go to that and come—"

"I have to be in New York the day after Christmas to meet with the new ad agency. You know how important hiring that agency is for me. I cannot change it and I need time with the team to prepare."

She inched back, more from the force of his words than any real disappointment. She always knew this would be the answer. She knew she wouldn't come back today and mysteriously find the husband she wished she had.

She sighed, and surrendered to that. "Okay, so you'll be gone most of the month anyway. Then I'll go with Brooke."

He gave her a sharp look, clearly not expecting that. "You think she's going to want to leave and go, um, hiking?" He snorted a laugh. "Have you met our daughter?"

She grunted at the insult, gutted by it. By every word and every look that made her feel small and unwanted and...wrong. "Stop it, Craig. Just stop being so mean, will you?"

"I'm not being mean, Angie. But I guarantee you, Brooke will not want to go with you."

"Depends." Brooke floated into the kitchen, walking without looking up from her phone, a literal extension of her body. "Is it shopping? I could be talked into it." She lowered the phone, revealing a delicate face with way too much eyeliner and soft, dark waves brushing her cheekbones. "But no Black Friday leftover garbage. I can't be bothered with those people trampling each other to save fifty bucks on a laptop."

She took a few steps closer, giving Angie a chance to see she wore a crop top and denim shorts that could possibly be classified as underwear, but now was not the time for a lecture.

Momentarily, Angie wondered just how much of that conversation Brooke had really heard, and if she had any concept of how broken her parents' marriage was. Not that she had a concept of anything these days, besides social media and disappearing with her new sketchy friends and the boyfriend who didn't know the meaning of eye contact.

Craig used the break in their conversation to escape toward his office down the hall as Angie plastered on a smile for her daughter.

"Hello to you, sweetheart. Did you have a nice Thanksgiving?"

She shrugged and looked at her phone. "Vance's family is super extra about it, but yeah, it was cool. Where did you want to go?"

"Asheville," Angie said. "For Christmas. Actually, for the entire month of December, but you might have to clear that with your teachers before break. Maybe take any end of semester tests online."

Brooke didn't respond, her thumbs and their chipped dark blue nail polish flying a mile a minute as she typed a text on the phone.

"Brooke," Angie prodded, waiting for her to look up.

"Yeah. I'm listening," she said flatly, still typing. "What did you say about tests online?"

"Please put your phone down and listen to me."

"I can do two things at once, Mom." She did lower it an inch, but kept her gaze on the screen.

"You know your Great-Aunt Elizabeth, right?"

Brooke looked up, her interest piqued. "Um, yeah. She brought me a Prada wallet directly from Milan last time she visited. Is she coming again?"

Angie tried not to cringe at the materialism. Somehow it was endearing with Noelle, who worked tirelessly for her luxury indulgences, but annoying with an entitled teenager.

"Uh, no. We're going to see her. For a month, for all of December."

She processed that, her expression shifting from shock to interest to the face she made when she knew her frenemies were going to get jealous. "In Europe? Sweet."

"No, in, um…" Angie took a breath. "In *Asheville*."

"Nashville? Like…the country music place?"

Seriously? "Asheville," she repeated. "At my family's North Carolina cabin for Christmas."

Brooke curled her lip so hard, she looked like a fish getting pulled by a hook. "Um, since when do we have a cabin?"

"Well, I never mention it because it's almost always rented out. Aunt Elizabeth owns it, since she's the last member of my mother's family. I used to go there as a kid during holidays and summertime, and I think you'd really enjoy it. Especially at Christmas when it's just beautiful."

Brooke gave a soft, sarcastic laugh. "Um, yeah, some creepy cabin on the other side of the universe sounds fun and all, but, sorry. I already told Vance's mom I'd spend Christmas with them."

Angie flinched at the impact of that, at the fact that her family was so fractured her sixteen-year-old daughter would choose to spend Christmas with her boyfriend's parents. Talk about failure as a parent and as a wife. Angie was *drowning* in it.

"Vance's family, huh?" She tried to play it cool.

"Yeah, they have a place in Tahoe. It's sick."

Of course they did. Vance, whose father was the CEO of a tech company, had blown into Brooke's life at the beginning of the school year. Three months later, her daughter was as unrecognizable to Angie as Craig had become.

Vance and his friends had money—big, fat, do-anything-you-want kind of money—and way too much freedom. The change in Brooke had been fast and furious as she'd shifted from a fun, sometimes sarcastic, wonderfully intelligent sophomore last year to a bitter, scowling, desperate-to-fit-in junior this year.

Angie danced around all the ways she could respond and decided she didn't want to fight this. If Brooke did go to North Carolina, she'd make everyone's life miserable. She'd think Eve's boys were weird and uncool, she'd be bored silly in the mountains, and, truth be told, they didn't know what they'd find out was going on with Aunt Elizabeth.

Maybe Tahoe with the...whatever-their-last-name-was family might be better. "Are you sure Vance's family doesn't mind you coming along for the holidays? We can offer to pay for your meals and—"

"Mom." Brooke shot her a look. "His parents love me and they're super chill. You don't have to get all weird about it."

Oh, *his* parents loved her. What about *her* parents?

Crushed by the weight of failures, Angie shut her eyes and stepped back. "So, if I stay here, I'll be alone for Christmas and my birthday, since you and Dad will both be gone."

She waited for Brooke to feel a pang of guilt, a shred of emotion about ditching her mother on Christmas and her birthday, but no such feeling surfaced.

Instead, Brooke walked back up the stairs, her eyes fixed downward on the phone screen. "You should go," she managed to mutter.

Angie leaned against the island, tears stinging her eyes.

What she would give to have been able to spend her sixteenth Christmas with her mom was incalculable, but Brooke had no concept of that kind of pain. And Angie wouldn't want her to.

She walked around the island and opened the refrigerator door, grabbing a bottle of Evian and twisting off the top. It was cool and refreshing as she sipped it, gazing out to the browns and blues of California, a place that had never felt like home.

Home was a place far away, a distant memory of the past. Home was Eve's sweetness and Noelle's focus, all brought together by Aunt Elizabeth's eccentric fabulosity.

Like her sisters, Angie hadn't been back to the cabin since that last Christmas, twenty-five years ago. So, if she did go, she was in for some serious emotions.

She was ready, though, and she knew how desperately she needed some sort of change, or breakthrough in her life.

"It's settled, then," Angie whispered to herself, wiping away one single tear that slipped down her cheek. "I'm going alone."

Chapter Three

Eve

EVE WAITED until the morning they were going to leave to tell the boys. She'd even let them start their schoolwork that day, even though she knew they'd be leaving soon after David did his morning rounds and saw two patients at his office.

But it was time to pack, so she headed up to the large loft they'd turned into a classroom, pausing at the top of the stairs to take in the three desks, an art project area, a computer section, a floor-to-ceiling bookshelf, and a storage wall—a work of alphabetized art that could bring a neat freak like Eve to happy tears.

That neat freak was about to burst into *un*happy tears, because the classroom looked like a tornado had gone through it. A tornado named Sawyer.

"Don't be upset, Mom." Bradley, her middle child, beamed up at her with far too much wisdom and patience for an almost-eight-year-old. "I'll help you clean it."

Letting out a whimper of love, she reached for him.

"We can do a quickie clean, honey," she said. "I have something exciting to tell you guys."

"We're on break?" Sawyer shot up from the desk he abhorred, zooming to her. "Thank you! Can I play? I'll be outside!" As he whizzed by, she managed to snag him by the threads of his Mario Bros. T-shirt.

"Hang on, cowboy."

"Mom, please! Ten minutes? I'll die if I can't breathe." He put his hand on his chest and pretended to hyperventilate. "I need *air!*"

She tried not to laugh, but it was impossible. "You need to help clean this room."

He collapsed to the floor. "Air, I tell you!"

"Let him go, Mom," Bradley said on a sigh of pure sainthood. "I can clean up his mess. What's the exciting thing you wanted to tell us?"

She glanced around, almost physically unable to make any announcement in this chaos.

"Are you done yet, James?" she called to her oldest boy, who had a headset on and stared at the computer screen, his mouth moving as he practiced his Spanish lesson.

He held up his hand, splaying out five fingers. "*Cinco minutos, Mamacita!*"

She smiled and let go of Sawyer. "You heard the man," she whispered. "Play outside for *cinco minutos.* In that time, do not sprain your wrist, skin your knee, or break a bone."

"No promises!" And with that, he was gone, disappearing down the hall, through the kitchen, and, presumably, out the back door.

"And I'll clean," Bradley said, heading to his desk.

"Thank you, bud."

Eve dove in, too, picking up some supplies as she thought about how they'd react to the news. She'd saved the announcement until the very last moment out of self-preservation more than the desire to surprise them. She knew the minute they found out they were going to the mountain cabin for a month, they'd be jumping out of their skins with anticipation and not a single school assignment would be completed.

At ages eleven, seven, and six, James, Bradley, and Sawyer were dream sons any way she cut it. With wildly different personalities and even looks, her boys were bright, brilliant, athletic, and outgoing, and there didn't seem to be an activity they didn't want to tackle.

Eve was partially to blame for that, since her decision to homeschool had her worried they wouldn't get the right amount of socialization. As a result, she signed them up for, well, everything. Little did she know they'd end up loving, well...*everything*.

Between swimming, baseball, theater—who knew James could sing and act?—orchestra, soccer, and karate, all three boys were scheduled like they were senators, not students. Yes, it seemed like overkill and surely they'd start dropping some of the activities. When she wasn't supervising school, checking work, and planning the curriculum, she was whipping her minivan around town in one long clock-fighting, snack-making, schedule-producing balancing act.

If for no other reason, the month in Asheville would be an absolute dream. No practice, no games, no lessons, no laundry. Well, some laundry. They'd do some home-school, which would be easy, and all the outdoors they could handle.

In all honesty, Eve was more excited than they could ever be about this trip. She longed to return to that gorgeous mountain and make new memories with her family. She ached to share it all with David, who'd always wanted to go to this "mythical" log cabin, but knew it was, for all intents and purposes, off limits.

James whipped off his headset and spun around in the chair, his slightly crooked smile so much like David's, it never failed to touch Eve's heart. "*Estoy terminada.* Or *terminado.* I don't know-o, but I'm done. What up, fam?"

"I'm going to get Sawyer," she said. "You two, do not move. This is big."

"Big like...we're going to a movie tonight 'cause Dad has to work?" James asked. "Or big like you finally found the new PlayStation console and you won't make us wait for Christmas?"

"Big like..." She grinned at him. "Huge."

Bradley and James shared a wide-eyed look while Eve pivoted and went downstairs to see where the Wild Thing was.

On a scooter in the driveway, it turned out.

"Mommy, watch this!" He jumped off the scooter

and flung it around, clumsily hopping back on it and kicking his feet to get another start.

"That's amazing, hon. Can we come back inside for just a few minutes? Big news time!"

"This *is* big news!" He flipped the scooter again and stumbled, falling to a knee. "I'm good, I'm cool!" he called out before Eve could run toward him.

"You sure?"

He looked down at his knee, visible in shorts even though it was really sweatpants weather. "No blood!"

A minor victory. "Come on, kiddo. Back inside."

Thankfully, wild Sawyer with his bouncing mane of chocolate curls and giant, giddy grin, went bounding back into the house, leaping through the entryway.

It was a miracle that child had never broken a bone. Not yet, anyway.

Back in the homework room, Eve got them settled in a group and sat down on her favorite beanbag chair, which was the size of a small country and perfect for reading with one or two boys snuggled up next to her.

"Okay, listen to me for a minute, please. Your life is about to change."

That got their attention, giving her the rare blessed moment of all three pairs of eyes on her. Until Sawyer grabbed a marker and started coloring on a random scrap of paper, but Eve decided to let it go for now.

"We are about to take a trip."

"We're going to Disney World!" Sawyer yelled, shooting his marker in the air.

"Um, no. Even better."

He drew back, shocked that something could be better.

"We're going to Asheville for a month at my family's mountain cabin."

"A month in the mountains?" James asked.

"That's cool, Mom," Bradley said, nodding as if he approved.

"We're going to Ashtray!" Sawyer yelled.

She waited a minute before answering, mentally noting that each of her boys had stayed true to character. One serious and analytical, one sweet and endearing, one...ridiculous.

"I didn't know we could go to that cabin," James said. "Dad says it's a rental."

"It was, but Aunt Elizabeth has invited us all there for the whole month of December," she told them. "We'll celebrate Christmas there and you can hike, and play, and cut down the Christmas tree."

"Cut down a tree?" James fist pumped. "Su-weet."

"I love to hike," Bradley added.

But little Sawyer was suddenly—weirdly—quiet. His eyes grew big as he stared at her.

"Sawyer?" Eve asked. "Good news, huh?"

"What about...you know..." He averted his gaze, clearly not wanting to say whatever was on his mind.

"I *don't* know. Can you enlighten me?"

"Well..." He sighed. "Will there be...Christmas presents?"

"Of course!" she replied with a laugh. "You think I'd

forget..." Oh. She knew exactly what he was thinking and why he wouldn't say it out loud.

Santa. He believed...but he didn't. Six was an "on the cusp" age, especially with an eleven-year-old brother who wasn't so good at playing the Santa game.

"It'll be fine, bud. I promise."

He looked a little unsure.

Next to him, James rolled his eyes and tried not to laugh. Eve gave him a harsh look, but of course, it was tender-hearted Bradley who leaned closer to his little brother.

"Santa can find you anywhere, Soy-sauce. No worries."

Sawyer relaxed, his face a little flushed. "'Kay. Cool beans."

"It is cool," she agreed. "You will most definitely still get presents. But what's important is that we're going to be with family. Aunt Noelle, Aunt Angie, and your Great-Aunt Elizabeth."

"Aunt Elizabeth." Bradley's brown eyes widened and glistened with the mention of their great-aunt, who was more of a fairy godmother than an actual relative.

"She brings candy!" Sawyer asserted loudly. "Chocolate from Bel-gum!"

"Belgium," Eve corrected with a soft laugh. "Yes, she certainly does bring quite the array of gifts."

"And Dad?" James asked. "He's coming for a whole month?" His face actually lit up at the idea of spending so much time with David, making Eve's heart fold. She felt the same hope he did.

"He's going with us and will try to be there as much as possible," she said. "It's only three hours away, so he's working on his schedule to get big blocks of time free."

"Yes!" James fist pumped again, his adoration of his father on full display.

"When are we leaving?" Bradley asked.

"As soon as you're packed and Dad's home."

The two younger ones nearly exploded, popping up in shock and the unspoken need to move.

"Whoa, whoa, wait a second." James stopped them all. "What about school, Mom?"

"Well, that's the beauty of homeschooling, bud," she assured him. "We can do it while we're at the cabin. Plus, you guys are so ahead that we're able to relax the schedule a bit for the holidays. I want to really enjoy this time as a family, you know? Get away from everything and have a real, true, family Christmas in the mountains."

"And soccer?" James pressed, his cornsilk hair falling around his face. "And I have the Christmas pageant."

She winced a little, dreading this announcement. "I was hoping that since you have a big play this spring, you might skip the pageant this year."

She waited for a flash of disappointment, but he nodded, the picture of maturity. "I've done the pageant three years in a row. It's fine, Mom."

"Thank you, honey."

"But I have violin lessons and Sawyer and I both have karate," Bradley added.

"I know, I know." Eve held up her hand. "Believe me, I'm very familiar with the schedule." Her mind flashed with an image of the whiteboard calendar hanging in the kitchen, covered in different-colored scribbles and markings denoting every activity, practice, appointment, game, or event that one or all of the boys needed to attend.

Eve had, of course, already considered this and carefully weighed the pros and cons of taking such a long Christmas getaway when her boys were so deeply involved in various activities.

Since the decision was made on Thanksgiving, she'd had almost a week to plan everything out, contact all of their coaches and instructors and directors, and everyone agreed that things were slow enough in December that they could miss it.

"We're taking a little break from everything," she said, taking a deep breath because the words sounded so good just to say. "I know you all have a lot going on, and every single thing you do is very important to me and your father. But we've decided that this trip is worth sacrificing a few weeks of activities, and I promise you that you won't be missing out on anything critical. You can play soccer in the grounds at the cabin and bring your violin to practice in Asheville."

"Great." James rolled his eyes and elbowed Bradley. "You can make that thing screech in any town."

Bradley shrugged, undaunted by the teasing. "Fine by me. I want to go hiking and make s'mores."

"Or snowmen, if it snows," Eve said, feeling her heart lighten. They were just kids, after all. This overly intense world of team sports and exhausting schedules was probably taking as much of a toll on them as it was on her.

Which was why she knew this vacation was the right thing. The necessary thing.

"Is the cabin big?" James asked as they headed out of the homework room to pack.

"Does it have logs for walls?" Bradley chimed in.

"Will there be *bears*?" Sawyer asked, eyes wide.

Eve felt a smile pull. "Just let yourselves be surprised. I promise you're going to like it. Now go start packing! As soon as Dad comes home, we load up the cars."

The plan was that they'd drive to Asheville in two cars, so David could go back and forth for work. On the way, she'd swing by the regional airport and pick up both Noelle and Angie, who had somehow coordinated their last-minute flights to get in within a half-hour of each other. It was true Christmas magic, they'd jokingly decided.

As they ran up the stairs with the noise of a buffalo herd, she waited at the bottom, giving them time to start their own packing. She'd have to supervise the packing process, of course, likely doing all of it herself, but she decided to let them get started on their own.

In the meantime, she went into the kitchen to make some car snacks, checking the driveway for David's sedan. He'd pull into the garage any second.

She'd never needed a month away more, and he'd completely understood that. All she wanted was a long, relaxing, true family holiday where he didn't have to work long days or be on call the entire time.

She knew it was selfish to want those things. David saved lives, every single day. He was a good, hardworking doctor who dedicated his life and career to helping others. Many, many people needed him.

It just felt like sometimes, Eve and the boys needed him the most.

As she paced around the kitchen waiting to hear that garage door, her phone buzzed with an incoming call.

Eve felt her heart sink instantly when she saw that it was David calling.

Please don't be running late. Please don't cancel. Please don't...

She sighed and regrouped, answering cheerfully. "Hey, honey! How close are you?"

"Eve, I'm so sorry."

She deflated instantly, biting back a groan. "What is it?"

"I have to stay at the hospital until late tonight. One of my surgery patients from yesterday is having complications with his recovery, and we may go back into the OR. It's urgent, so I've got to be here."

She bit back her disappointment, too used to this to be surprised. "I'll just let my sisters know and we'll leave in the morning. It's—"

"I can't, Eve. I got scheduled for seven-thirty AM surgery I cannot change. I'll have to meet you guys a few days later, since I've got that craniectomy on Tuesday. You should go today as planned."

"Oh, no." Eve pressed her hand to her chest, always feeling sympathy for the patients and family of people who were going through something far more serious than her...life. That's what complicated this. She couldn't get mad at him for working so hard—lives literally depended on this man and his incredible surgical skills. "Of course. I completely understand."

"You told the boys, huh? They're amped up?"

She could hear his smile through the phone, visualizing his strong features and kind eyes, his hair completely covered by a teal surgical cap. David always tied his wedding band to the drawstrings of his scrubs when he went into surgery, and she knew it was hanging there now, a piece of her with him.

"They're thrilled, and I know how much they're going to love the cabin. It's so magical at Christmastime. I really hope we can find that magic this year."

David chuckled. "I never pegged your Aunt Elizabeth as one for Christmas magic. You're absolutely sure this whole thing was her idea?"

"It was all in the email, as bizarre as can be."

"Well, give the boys a hug for me, okay? You guys go and I'll find my way to that cabin as soon as I can. Definitely by Friday night. I promise. Weekends are yours, babe, and the last two weeks of the month, all the way to early January. I have it off and nothing can change that."

Eve clenched her jaw and fought her disappointment.. "Okay. You promise?"

"What's that? Sorry, honey, you cut out."

Eve swallowed, speaking louder into the phone speaker. "I just asked if you prom—"

"Oh, sorry, I've got to go. Love you, hon. Talk later."

The line clicked off and Eve set her phone down on the countertop, exhaling a huff of sadness.

He was doing everything he could. When they married and he was in medical school, she knew he'd have a demanding job as a family doctor. But as he progressed in school, and specialized, and eventually focused on neurosurgery, that job became beastly. He had long, exhausting hours that left him little time for family.

Sometimes, she wished he had stuck with being a family doctor. That was okay. Their marriage was wonderful, except so much of it was spent...missing him.

Eve feared their connection was slipping away, their closeness in jeopardy of disappearing completely with the craziness of their lives.

Which was exactly why this unexpected Christmas trip meant so much to her. She hoped so badly that they could reconnect, feel the magic of family and the holiday and the beauty of their wonderful sons, but Eve feared there was no such possibility.

It was all right, she told herself. He was doing his best. And as for her? She headed up the stairs to control each item the boys packed in their suitcases, because that was what *she* did best. Control.

Or, more accurately, attempt to control, and then fail. But that would never stop Eve from trying.

"Okay, kiddos. Let's see what we're working with here." She reached the top of the stairs and went into Sawyer's room first.

He'd filled a backpack to the brim with Legos and Hot Wheels cars and plastic dinosaur figurines, and was grinning wildly as he shoved more toys into the bag. "I'm packing, Mommy!"

Eve sighed and perched on the edge of his bed, pulling his little suitcase out from underneath the bed, preparing to handle this. To handle everything, as she always did. Alone, missing her other half.

One day at a time, she thought to herself. All she could do was take life one day at a time, and knowing she was about to spend Christmas in the mountains with her sisters made everything better.

Chapter Four

Noelle

As Eve cruised along the winding, scenic turns of the Blue Ridge Parkway in her minivan, Noelle sat in the seat behind her, leaning her head against the window. Emotion gripped her throat as she gazed out at the endless rolling layers of mountains, the thick trees that covered them were mostly bare now, but the far mountains still looked blue.

Eve, as promised, had been waiting at the Asheville Regional Airport for both Noelle and Angie, wearing a giddy smile and patiently, gently corralling her rowdy bunch of boys.

James, Bradley, and Sawyer were all packed in the "way" back, simultaneously ooh-ing and ahh-ing at the breathtaking views and each crazy turn that had them close to the edge of the mountains.

Angie, in the front passenger seat, was quiet, her mood noticeably as blue as the mountain range. With unspoken understanding, they knew they'd discuss all matters of life once they were reunited with Aunt Elizabeth and could have true quality time.

"I saw a bear!" Sawyer screamed suddenly. "Right there in those trees, then he was gone."

James sighed. "You didn't see a bear, Sawyer."

"Yeah-huh, I did!" Sawyer insisted, and Noelle bit back a laugh at his wild attitude and palpable sass. "It was a big one, Mommy. I swear it."

"Totally possible." Eve lifted a slender shoulder as she took the next bend, giving Noelle a shot of déjà vu as she remembered Dad taking them for joyrides in the summer.

Yikes. Was the whole month going to be one long trip down memory lane?

Noelle inhaled at the thought, bracing as some icy nostalgia crept up her spine, a mix of sweet history and deep pain. Coming back here, to this town, to these mountains...it was a confusing cocktail of emotions that she was determined to conquer.

And, in fact, it was hard to be anything but happy with Eve's trio of entertainment in the back of the van, arguing about a mythical bear.

"Mom, have you ever seen a bear here?" James demanded. "I'm sure they're around, but there's no way it was that close to the road."

"It was, James!" Sawyer practically bounced in his seat and leaned into the space next to Noelle's seat. "I looked him right in the eyes." He pointed his two fingers at his face, then at the imaginary bear, squinting into the distance. "I let him know who's boss."

Of course she laughed. How could you not with this kid?

Angie turned around in the passenger seat with a smile. "Actually, black bears are all over this area, and they're even friendlier than you'd expect," she said. "We used to see them all around the cabin when we were kids."

Noelle was relieved to see a spark from her sister, who'd been so quiet since they'd met up at the airport.

Bradley, James, and Sawyer all gasped in unison as their eyes widened.

"It's true," Noelle chimed in. "They're everywhere. But they won't bother you if you don't bother them, as your Grandpa Jim would say."

The three sisters exchanged a look, connected by the memory of how much Dad loved coming to these mountains. For him, it was a break from the life of being a college English professor at NC State. Here, he would don his flannel in winter to chop wood for the fireplace, and wear his cringeworthy tank tops for hours of fishing in the summer.

Dad had a bounce in his step when they were in the mountains, and seemed to love his "trilogy"—as the literature fanatic liked to call his daughters—with even more passion here than when they were at home in Raleigh.

"Bears are scary even if you leave them alone," Bradley said, clearly the least alpha of Eve's own trilogy.

"Scary?" Sawyer scoffed. "I'm not scared. I want one as a pet. I could train it to do tricks."

"Slow down there, Cesar Millan," Eve warned with a soft laugh. "There will be no bear whispering on this vacation. Keep your eyes out, boys. We're almost at the cabin."

With Eve's announcement, the car went silent as all six of them were captivated by the views, which grew more and more stunning as they left the highway and started to round the base of the area known as Copper Creek.

Farms spread out over the foothills, with quaint houses and wide-open acres dotted with cows, sheep, horses, and the occasional llama out from their stables. As they climbed higher, a dusting of white snow added contrast and magic to everything—the trees seemed taller up here, and the air thinner.

Noelle held her breath when Eve took the exit onto Creekside Road, not sure she was prepared for what new emotions would well up when they reached the long gravel driveway that led to the cabin.

"You guys ready?" Eve asked, presumably to her boys, but the question was indirectly pointed at Angie and Noelle, too.

Noelle swallowed, not knowing the answer.

"Mmm." Angie's response was noncommittal, making Noelle suspect the same doubt, fear, and anticipation swirled through her.

Noelle leaned forward and put a hand on each of her sisters' shoulders. "Hey, you two. We Chambers girls can handle anything, right?"

Angie just smiled, but Eve tilted her head to get it closer to Noelle's fingertips.

"That's what Dad would say," she whispered. "And he'd want us to be happy today."

"So would Mom," Angie added.

Noelle squeezed their shoulders. "Then we are."

It had been twenty-five long years since they'd been on Creekside Road, and when they left, they'd been shattered. The trees along the drive had been plenty bare that day, except for the red pop of winterberry that bloomed at the last curve, right where you could see—

"The red mailbox is still there!" Eve exclaimed.

"Then that's the turn." Angie leaned forward, excitement finally in her voice.

As the van crunched over the driveway that meandered toward the cabin, Noelle shut her eyes for one last second. She let one hand fall to the leather console in between the driver's and front passenger's seats, not surprised when Angie and Eve placed their hands on top of hers.

The three of them squeezed their fingers together in a moment of fear, hope, sadness and prayer.

"It's so crazy being back here," Noelle said quietly, feeling her heart rate pick up as she waited for the cabin to come into view.

"Understatement of the century," Angie murmured.

They followed the creek, the split-rail fence, the last three pine trees...and there it was.

· · ·

PERCHED on a rise halfway up the mountain, tucked into trees, the Asheville cabin stood with as much grace, warmth, and hope as Noelle remembered.

"It's huge," James exclaimed.

"It's really nice," Bradley added.

"It's made of honest-to-goodness logs!" Sawyer practically shrieked with joy.

It was all those things, Noelle thought as she gazed at the beautiful structure through misty eyes. It looked as lovely as she remembered, with tall dormers, large windows, and a huge wooden deck that spread like welcoming arms from every corner of the house.

Raised on tall beams above the basement and piles of stacked wood, seven wide steps led up to the front door, beckoning visitors to a cabin that was everything she hoped it would be, and more.

"Wow." Eve let out a breath of relief. "Someone has taken very good care of this place."

"You're right," Angie agreed, sounding as surprised. "I expected it to be ramshackle and rundown."

"Aunt Elizabeth wouldn't let that happen," Noelle said as the realization dawned. "She might not have come here—or at least if she did, she didn't tell us—but it's clear she's maintained this property with love and care."

The wood gleamed in the afternoon sun—yes, they were real logs, with knotty pine on every wall inside. The windows had been replaced over the years, and...was that a new roof? Every spindle in the deck railing was in perfect condition and the split-rail that wrapped around the front yard was new.

A wash of gratitude filled Noelle as she took it all in.

"I'm so glad she did that," Angie said, her voice thick with emotion, her thoughts obviously following Noelle's. "Because she didn't have to."

"She loved this place as much as Mom did," Eve said. "Even though..." Her voice trailed off and she cleared her throat. "So, what do you think, boys?" she asked brightly as she turned off the ignition. "Want to spend a month here?"

The answer was low-key chaos and a chorus of, "Yes!" as they eagerly unlatched seatbelts and wiggled their way to freedom and the joys of cabin life.

"Let's go!" James pleaded, pushing the empty seat next to Noelle so he could get to the door.

He flicked the release and it slid open, filling the van with chilly, fresh air.

"Help with the bags, please!" Eve managed, but three small bodies were jumping out like skydivers eager to fall to the ground.

Noelle, Eve, and Angie sat alone for a quick, quiet second.

"You guys ready?" Noelle asked softly, leaning forward to look back and forth between her two dear sisters.

"Of course." Eve nodded. "We're going to have a blast."

Angie lifted a shoulder and glanced at Noelle. "If Eve Gallagher declares it, then it must be true."

On that note of reassurance, they opened their car doors and stepped onto the gravel, stomping their boots and rubbing their arms against the refreshing mountain air.

Angie dropped her head back, her burnished gold curls falling over her shoulders. "I love being back here!"

"Me, too," Eve agreed, looking around.

"Everything is exactly the same," Noelle sighed, so happy about that.

"Uh...well..." Eve's whole expression changed as she stared over Noelle's shoulder toward the cabin. "Not...*everything*."

Noelle turned to follow Eve's shocked gaze, blinking in the afternoon sun, certain it had to be playing tricks on her.

Who was that woman coming down the stairs?

Was that...could it be...no! There was no way. For a moment, Noelle's whole world tilted as she stared at a woman who couldn't, in any universe, be her Aunt Elizabeth.

And then the woman called out to them and Noelle recognized her voice. But everything else about Elizabeth Whitaker was completely and totally different.

HUGS AND HELLOS, along with unloading luggage and lots of little boy commotion, took enough time that Noelle could catch her breath and accept that this imposter was, after all, the real Elizabeth Whitaker, a fashion icon who'd taught her to "never, ever show up at the airport looking like a ragamuffin."

But hadn't this very woman—the one in filthy boots—taught her "the most elegant outfit begins and ends with the right shoes"? Noelle glanced down at her Louboutins, which suddenly seemed like she'd taken the travel advice a step too far.

And what about, "A woman's hair is her crowning glory"? Noelle had heard that a million times.

But Aunt Elizabeth's signature auburn blunt cut with coppery highlights and chin-length tapering was now... silver. Long hair falling from a careless ponytail framed a face that could only be called...radiant.

Crow's feet and brow lines that had been kept at bay for years with Botox were noticeable and natural. Without shadow, her eyes seemed to shimmer from the inside and her smile—even without her favorite shade of deep red lipstick—beamed as bright as the sun overhead.

"My sweet Noelle." Elizabeth stepped forward for a second hug, this one tighter than the first, her outpouring of love palpable.

Did it matter that she'd changed? This was still one of Noelle's favorite humans alive. Noelle leaned into the embrace, only a little sad not to get a whiff of Chanel No. 5, the scent she always associated with her aunt. Today, she smelled like sunshine and pine and...maybe a...cow? Something not found at the Bergdorf fragrance counter.

"Oh, Aunt Elizabeth." Noelle gave one last squeeze before pulling away, looking over her shoulder at Eve and

Angie to see if they seemed as perplexed as she was. But Eve was giving luggage orders to the boys and Angie was looking around, taking everything in. "What an incredible surprise," Noelle finished, not sure what to say.

The other woman drew back, her blue eyes glinting with a tease. "Coming here or seeing the new me?"

Noelle laughed. At least she was still direct and candid. "Both, if I have to be honest."

"I expect you to always be honest, Lambchop."

The endearment from so long ago touched Noelle's heart. "Then you better have a great explanation."

"So great," she assured Noelle, then reached for Angie. "Now, come in, all of you. Let those big boys handle all the baggage and figure out the bedrooms. We'll just switch everything to the way we want it later."

Eve laughed and gave their aunt a kind smile. "Thank you so much for this invitation. The boys are just over the moon about being here, and we're all..."

"Wondering why you're here," Elizabeth finished with a quick laugh. "We'll get to that soon enough. Right now, I just want to hold you three angels and thank the good Lord I have you in my life. I'm beyond blessed."

She closed her eyes for a quick second and Noelle could have sworn she was...praying? Was that *possible*?

With that, she led them up the stairs and into the house, which was as upgraded and well-kept inside as it was on the outside.

"Settle in right here." Elizabeth kicked off her hideous boots, revealing red fuzzy socks, and gestured to the cozy sectional in front of the fireplace.

Like its current owner, the inside of the cabin was all different—simple and rustic, but still achingly welcoming.

As Eve gushed about how gorgeous the place looked, Angie peeked into the sunroom that spilled from the kitchen and gave them a year-round patio that overlooked the mountains beyond. But Noelle crossed her arms and stayed put, waiting impatiently for the promised explanation.

"Girls, girls, come by the fire." Aunt Elizabeth beckoned them to sit. "Can I get you anything? Hot cocoa? I've been just completely loving myself a hot cocoa ever since the weather got chilly."

Hot cocoa? Aunt Elizabeth drank dry martinis, for lunch and dinner.

Whoever this woman was, she sure seemed happy and sweet. But it wasn't Aunt Elizabeth, and the clearer that became, the more concern started to churn in Noelle's gut.

What if she really *was* sick? What if she was living out some sort of dying wish to have one more Christmas at the cabin? What if doctors said she couldn't color her hair or wear makeup or she had some illness that forced her to dress like a...scarecrow?

After they all politely passed on beverages, Elizabeth finally got them all on the sofa as she stood in the center of the room like a teacher about to start class. She took a deep breath, looking at each of them.

"Now, let's talk." With that, she folded onto the ottoman in the middle, crossing her overall-covered legs with her red socks sticking out, a few unkempt silver hairs falling from the clip. "Well, *I'll* talk. You line up your questions."

Eve laughed and Angie leaned forward, fascinated. Noelle just sat very, very still, not sure how she felt at all.

"I'm well aware that there's a large elephant stomping around this room right now," Elizabeth began. "Starting with, 'Why did I invite you here when we've avoided this very place and this very holiday for twenty-five years?' Or perhaps you're wondering why I've changed a few things about my appearance, or maybe why I'm not in some fabulous, faraway place for Christmas."

"How about all of the above?" Angie quipped.

Eve nodded, looking over at her sisters then back at their aunt. "I can't lie, Aunt Elizabeth. We were all confused by the invitation. Excited, and overjoyed, but...confused."

Noelle wanted to scream, "Who are you and where did you hide my precious aunt?" but the words lodged in her throat.

"Of course you were confused, and I don't blame you one bit." Elizabeth sighed. "Now, let me answer your questions and put your minds and hearts at ease. First and foremost, my life has changed."

Noelle practically writhed on the sofa, hearing the words of a therapist she'd seen for ten years echo in the back of her head.

You, Noelle Chambers, hate change.

Oh, she did. Hated it with a passion. Change always

meant...loss. Had she lost her beloved aunt? Was she about to?

"For one thing," Elizabeth said, looking directly at Noelle, "I've fully retired."

Noelle exhaled. Okay. Retirement. The woman had worked hard and was in her sixties. She deserved to retire.

Proud of herself for easily accepting this change, Noelle nodded. "Good for you, Aunt Elizabeth. You've earned it."

"Obviously, I've come back here," she continued, gesturing around the cabin. "And made some improvements."

"It looks beautiful," Eve said sincerely.

"Thank you, honey. But there's more."

Please, just don't be sick. I can't lose you, too.

"I've also had quite a change of...spirit," she said on a laugh. "After a lifetime of believing I was my own boss, I realized..." She pointed upward. "There is a much higher power."

Oh. Noelle leaned back, letting this news sink in. *All right, all right. Everyone's entitled to their beliefs.* And she imagined as a person neared their golden years, they gave a lot more thought to the afterlife.

"That's lovely," Angie said softly.

"But the biggest change of all is what prompted all of this," Elizabeth said.

Oh, boy, Noelle thought. *Here it comes.* The diagnosis. The bad news. The worst change of all. She braced her whole body for the words, but Aunt Elizabeth was staring at all of them with dancing eyes and a smile that reminded Noelle of a child on, well, Christmas morning.

"I'm in love!" she exclaimed, throwing both hands in the air.

"What?" Angie asked.

Eve gasped. "You've met someone?"

"You're...in love?" Noelle's question caught in her throat, this last revelation the most surprising of all.

Her sisters peppered the room with questions but Noelle remained completely quiet, letting this news sink in.

With the exception of a few fascinating and wealthy clients who'd tried to woo her, Elizabeth Whitaker was the most anti-love woman alive. She lived and breathed independence and the power of self and the thrill of steering your own life in the exact direction you want it to go without a man to tell you how, when, or where.

"Where's he from?" Angie asked. "Because knowing you, he's Greek, has a yacht, and is taking us all in his private plane to the Mediterranean."

Elizabeth laughed. "He lives ten minutes down the road on his farm. You passed it coming up the mountain, with the silo and all the land."

"He's a...farmer?" Noelle managed to croak.

"He's a prince—"

Oh, that made sense.

"Among men," she finished. "He's shown me the beauty in simplicity, the wonder of real, deep roots, and more than that, the light of the Lord." Her eyes grew misty, and Noelle's heart tugged in about eight different directions. "He's changed my whole life, girls. And I just heard his truck pull up, so you all wait here, digest the news, and brace yourselves to meet the man who has changed my life."

For the longest time, Noelle just stared at her, and remembered how much she hated change.

Chapter Five

Eve

"Mom!"

"Mommy!"

"*Mamacita!*"

Eve laughed as the various names came along with heavy footsteps down the stairs the moment Aunt Elizabeth left. Sawyer was first, no surprise, flying into the living room.

"There's a dog!" he hollered. "Outside! An actual dog! In a truck! I saw him!"

"No doubt he comes with the farmer," Noelle said wryly. "Perhaps he brought cows and sheep."

Eve looked at her sister and gave a sympathetic smile. "I can see all this has thrown you, Noelle."

"You think?"

"It's a lot," Angie agreed.

"Can we see the dog?" James asked, pointing outside. "Otherwise, Sawyer might implode."

"He's wanted a dog for a long time," Eve explained, reaching out a hand to her youngest. "Give Aunt Elizabeth a second to greet her guest."

"You think he's friendly?" Bradley asked warily, glancing toward the window.

"The dog or the farmer?" Noelle cracked.

"Hey." Angie elbowed her. "Give it a chance, okay?"

Eve stood, sensing she needed to talk Noelle off a ledge. Looking outside, she saw Aunt Elizabeth with her arms around a man in his sixties, gazing up at him like... well, like this was love.

A shiver of joy ran over Eve. "I'm so happy for her," she whispered.

"Because he has a dog?" Sawyer asked, bouncing on his little feet. "It's yellow! Can I go out and see it, please?"

Aunt Elizabeth and her...boyfriend—is that what they should call him?—parted and the man lowered the gate of his pickup and the dog leaped out.

"I think you can," she said. "But just be—"

Sawyer was halfway out the door before she finished, with James hot on his heels. Bradley lingered, giving Eve a worried look.

"Maybe they can just see if he's, you know, good with kids," he said.

"I'm sure he is." She gave him a gentle prod. "Why don't you go with them, honey?"

He took a step, hesitant. "I just, you know, haven't been around many dogs."

He'd been cautious around them since childhood for no apparent reason, but his wariness had been why she'd been able to say no to Sawyer's persistent begging. Maybe this would be a good chance to change that.

"Golden retrievers are friendly," she assured him.

"Just throw him a stick, Bradley," Angie said. "They're called 'retrievers' for a reason."

He smiled at that, nodding. "Okay. I'll go."

When he left, she turned to the others and dropped on the sofa with a sigh. "Well. We weren't expecting this, huh?"

Noelle gave a shaky laugh. "Uh, am I the only one slightly freaked out?"

"I think Bradley's a little uncertain," Angie said.

"About this new...romance," Noelle clarified.

Angie put a hand on her arm. "I know, hon. I'm just trying to keep it light for you."

"Light?" she scoffed. "The woman has undergone a complete personality change."

"Not really," Eve said. "She's the same person, just...I don't know. Really comfortable in her own skin? Letting herself age gracefully? Finding faith and love? I don't see what's wrong with any of that."

Noelle huffed out a sigh. "One minute she's my mentor, idol, and mother figure and the next, she's..."

"Going to be a farmer's wife," Eve offered, biting back a smile at the idea.

"Wife?" Noelle's voice rose. "Who said anything about getting *married*?"

"Does she have to?" Eve countered. "She's found God, she's in love, and I think that is the most natural place for them to go as a couple."

"No, no." Noelle shook her head. "I just think we're

being punked right now. Overalls and boots? Gray hair and...and...and a boyfriend?"

"Oh, Noelle." Eve reached out to her. "Aunt Elizabeth has found love and turned over a new leaf in life. There's nothing wrong with that. Look at her—she's glowing with happiness."

"She does seem happy," Noelle conceded. "But who changes that fast?" She looked at Angie for backup.

"I honestly don't know what to make of it," Angie said. "I'm reserving judgment, and I think you should, too, Noelle. I know this shakes your worldview."

"What does that mean?" Noelle asked, visibly struggling to keep her irritation in check.

"It means you have created a life that emulates hers, and that's been really good for you. But now she's changed her life and it rocks yours."

Noelle shrugged a shoulder, too smart to deny that.

"You want her to be happy, don't you?" Eve asked.

"Of course I do! I just don't want her to be...foolish." She arched a brow. "She's a successful woman with a very healthy bank account, if you get my drift."

Eve cringed at the implication. "You don't think...no. She's too smart to get swindled."

"She wouldn't be the first well-off woman in her sixties to turn over her savings to a man who wooed her off her feet."

"She is different, but not dumb," Angie said. "Come on, Noelle. Let's give her the love and support she's always given us."

"Of course I will," she said, wiping her hands on her

slacks and letting out another sigh. "I'm just naturally skeptical and protective of her."

"And that's fine." Angie scooted closer and put her arm around Noelle. "But I think she's happy, and I'm going to wait to meet—"

Just then, the front door opened and Elizabeth came in, her face bright with anticipation. Eve stood and so did her sisters. Right behind her, a man stepped in, his own smile as wide and sincere as Elizabeth's.

"Girls, this is Sonny McPherson. Sonny, meet the three angels who have blessed me since the day they were born."

"Wow, I've been waitin' for this," he said, easing off his shoes and taking off a Carolina Panthers ballcap in a move that was both respectful and endearing.

He was a fine-looking man in his mid- to late sixties with clear blue eyes and a complexion that looked like he'd spent many happy hours in the sun. His hair was light brown with gray temples and he wore faded jeans and a camo jacket over a T-shirt.

"This is Eve," Aunt Elizabeth said as she stepped forward and extended her hand. "Eve Gallagher, mother of those boys who just attached themselves to Lucky."

"You're raising mighty men of valor," he said with a laugh, giving her hand a solid shake with one that was callused and strong.

"I take it Lucky is your dog?" she guessed.

"He's my constant companion, so named because someone left him at my farm the day I had my first date with this sweet lady."

"Aww," Eve cooed. "So sweet."

"Hi, I'm Angie." She reached out for her turn to shake his hand.

He gave her a look as he took it, thinking. "Short for Angela?" he asked.

"Actually, Angel. We're Christmas babies, you know."

"Named for the heavenly hosts." His eyes widened. "I like that. Pleased to meet you, Angie."

Aunt Elizabeth stepped closer to Noelle and put a gentle arm around her. "And this is Noelle."

"Ah, the protégé," he said, nodding as they shook hands, his smile wavering ever so slightly, as if he knew she'd be the hard sell of the three. "Bitsy has told me so much about you."

Noelle's whole body seemed to freeze. "*Bitsy?*"

"Oh, yes." Aunt Elizabeth flicked her hand and rolled her eyes. "Gave me that silly little nickname when we first met."

Even Eve was stunned by this. "And you allowed it?"

"Not at first." Elizabeth lifted her chin. "But Sonny McPherson is a persistent man. In nicknames and in love, he knew what he wanted and eventually I just couldn't deny it anymore. He's simply the greatest man and has swept me off my feet."

Sonny flushed a little, casting his eyes down with a humble chuckle. "Couldn't let this one slip out of my hands."

"This one?" Noelle asked. "Have there been many?"

Eve shot her a warning look, but Elizabeth just laughed and elbowed Sonny.

"Told ya she'd be the challenge."

"I don't mean to challenge anything," Noelle said, although Eve didn't think she sounded very convincing about that. "I just wondered...you know...how many women have you swept off their feet?"

He angled his head and regarded her with warmth.

"One other," he said. "She gave me three beautiful children and a good many years, but she's with Jesus now. And I never dreamed I'd fall in love again, but..." He glanced at Elizabeth with nothing but adoration. "This sweet hurricane blew into my life and shook it all up."

They all laughed—well, maybe not Noelle, but even she had to thaw in the face of this dear man.

"I know it's a lot to take in," Sonny said, his thick Southern drawl icing every word like butter on a sticky bun. "But I promise, the love that your Auntie and I share is somethin' special, and we wanted y'all to come here to see it for yourselves."

He gestured them back to the sofa and took the loveseat next to Elizabeth, sitting down with his elbows on his knees. With his stocking feet and hat in hand, he looked utterly and completely...sweet. Like a suitor meeting the parents and wanting to make a good impression.

Well, Eve was definitely impressed, and her heart lifted as she settled in and smiled at him.

"We're so happy to be here," she assured him. "I'm sure you've heard it's been a long, long time."

"I know the story," he said, his smile disappearing. "And I'm touched that y'all came back to celebrate Christmas with us, which I hope gives us a chance to make all-new memories."

"Oh, we will!" Elizabeth interjected. "Starting with decorating! As long as you're all willing to help me set up all the old stuff, which is in the attic—and I'm personally not a fan of that space—we can deck the halls. Plus, there's the tree lighting in town and we'll have to cut down our own tree."

Sonny chuckled. "Let the girls settle in before you put them to work, Bitsy."

"We'd love to do all of that," Angie said.

"The boys will be all over the decorating project," Eve added.

"Are the decorations the same?" Noelle asked. "All of Mom and Dad's stuff? I know they kept them out here at the cabin."

Elizabeth nodded. "Yep, it's the ones you girls grew up with and I say it's about time they get put to use again, don't you agree?"

"I do," Eve said. "I think the best part of Christmas is bringing out the family favorites, and I know that attic has to have a lot of them."

Noelle took a deep breath, leaning in when the conversation stopped for a beat. "Aunt Elizabeth, when did you come back to the cabin? I thought you kept it rented out long-term and, well, to be honest, you did say you never wanted to come back."

"I've said a lot of things, sweetie." She inched to Sonny

and he draped an arm around her slender shoulders. "But our plans are not always...the right plans, you know?"

Noelle looked like she *didn't* know and Angie and Eve shared a quick look, but stayed silent.

"I actually did sneak back here over the years, once or twice. I mean, we have some sad memories, of course, but the cabin's been in my family for a long time and I felt a duty to keep it up. I checked on repairs and then we had longtime renters for about four years. They moved a year or so ago and reported some issues that needed to be fixed around the house. Big enough that I thought I should come and check it out myself."

"Isn't that when you considered selling the place?" Angie asked. "I seem to recall talking to you about it last winter."

"It was, but then I spent a week here last spring. Late February, actually. Just one week was all it took to sort of, well, let go. The cabin started to work its magic and I decided maybe I should update the place, and do some minor remodeling. Thought I might keep it for retirement and certainly offer it to you girls, since it's yours as much as mine. I spent the whole summer here and planned to finish by this past fall."

"You were here all this time?" Noelle asked, sounding put out by this information. "I thought you were traveling."

"I know you did, but I didn't want you girls to think about this cabin," she said. "I felt it was my responsibility to get it to the best condition it could be in. That was very important to your mother. And I love remodeling and decorating."

Eve looked around, really seeing all she'd done with the cabin, which had always been a little rustic but now was more...organic chic. No surprise, since Elizabeth had impeccable taste and—as Noelle had pointed out—a healthy bank account.

It was clear she'd refinished the floors, updated the kitchen, and had new windows installed. Even the fireplace looked spiffy, with a large TV mounted over it and well-considered art hanging everywhere.

"Anyway, I was here for a few months and it was April or so—"

"It was April eighteenth," Sonny interjected softly.

"That day," she continued, "I was poking around an antiques store in town and found that"—she pointed to a large weathered glass door in the kitchen that Eve knew led to what used to be a broom closet—"and I so desperately wanted to put new glass in the panels and use it as my pantry door. I was chatting with the store owner about that when this handsome man overheard and offered to help."

"I restore a little," he said. "And I have a truck, which, let's be honest, was just as important to her."

Elizabeth laughed. "He charmed me," she said, smiling at him. "Something about his...spirit."

"Oh, Bits." He shook his head.

"No, I mean it. I just felt something coming from inside him that was so...real. Next thing I knew, he was putting my door in his truck, getting my phone number and address—"

"That's when I found out we were neighbors, which, if you ask me, proved the good Lord has His mighty hands all over this."

Elizabeth laughed. "So, I got my door and I got..." She grinned at him. "My man."

"Is that when you started, um, wearing overalls?" Noelle asked. "Not they aren't very cute, Aunt Elizabeth, but..."

"Oh, child, I knew you'd have something to say about this fashion statement." Elizabeth gave a soft hoot and plucked at the denim. "Well, I couldn't run around his farm in high heels and a pencil skirt."

"But she had those heels on when I met her," he said. "Sky-high like the ladder in my barn. Cutest thing I ever saw. Course, I thought to myself, 'Now that's a fish out of water if I ever saw one.'"

"So you went fishing?" Noelle said with that dubious brow raised again.

"Well, I went courtin'," he corrected.

"And that worked?" Angie asked.

"Not quite." Elizabeth turned to Sonny and they laughed. "Despite the fact that he was the kindest, gentlest, sweetest man I'd ever met, I was still determined to stay true to my lifestyle and independence. After all, I didn't plan to stay here. I was going back to New York in the fall. But by then..." She sighed and dropped her head on Sonny's shoulder. "I was a goner."

"And I was the happiest man alive," he said. "I mean,

when you meet the most beautiful, brilliant angel that God ever made, you don't just let her slip away, and I didn't intend to. I set my sights on Bitsy and from our first date, I knew I was in love. She took a few months to catch up."

"Where did you go for your first date?" Eve asked, enchanted with the love story.

"Rocky's Hot Chicken Shack," Sonny said. "Best fried chicken east of the Mississippi and if you girls haven't been there, you're in for a treat."

"Aunt Elizabeth, you don't eat carbs," Noelle said with a soft, awkward laugh.

"Oh, well..." She shrugged. "I do now. Once you've tasted their spicy honey chicken thighs and homestyle potato salad, you'll be a changed woman, too. Trust me."

Angie laughed, shaking her head with as much disbelief as Noelle, but with much more amusement.

"So, do you plan on staying here?" Angie asked. "At the cabin?"

Elizabeth just beamed at Sonny. "I'm not going anywhere for the foreseeable future."

"And I couldn't be happier about that," Sonny added.

Noelle blinked at her, words trapped in her throat. "You're never coming back to New York?" she croaked.

"I know it's a shock, baby, I really do." Elizabeth gave Noelle an understanding smile. "But this is where we feel called in life, you know? I don't know how many years I've got left—none of us do. And Sonny and I don't want to waste another moment not being together."

He pulled her closer. "Amen to that, sweet Bitsy."

The front door popped open and the house was suddenly filled with three breathless boys and a barking dog.

"Lucky is the greatest dog ever!" Sawyer announced, his face flushed with color and damp with sweat despite the forty-degree temperature. "Can I have him, Uncle Sonny?"

Uncle Sonny? Well, he sure dove into this new normal with ease.

But Eve felt like she was right there with him and Angie looked like she could get on the Uncle Sonny wagon in no time. Noelle, however? Nope. That was not a happy camper, and Eve knew her sister would need some help to take that ride.

Well, they had a month. Anything could happen.

Chapter Six

Angie

JUST LIKE WHEN they were kids, Angie and Noelle picked the bedroom with twin beds that looked over the backyard, giving Eve the larger room with the queen-sized bed for when David was here. Aunt Elizabeth had transformed what had been a downstairs guest room and office into her beautiful master suite, so that left the boys to claim the third-floor loft area. They spread out over multiple bunks, and had a TV that it took no time at all to connect to their Nintendo Switch.

But they weren't interested in video games, hustling out to the yard after Aunt Elizabeth made them sandwiches, off to take Lucky for a walk and, as Sawyer whispered, "Go bear hunting!"

"Want to find Eve?" Angie asked as she came into the room from the hall bathroom. "I think she went downstairs to call David and let him know all the news."

Noelle already had her laptop open on her bed, her hair up in a scrunchy, and comfy sweats replaced her fancy traveling clothes. She looked up, her gaze distant.

"Are you seriously just...fine with all this?" she asked. "I mean, she's given up her life for a perfect stranger."

"I'm not going to try and talk her out of it, if that's what you mean." Angie came to the bed and sat on the edge. "I'll agree with perfect, but he's not a stranger. And she's so happy, Noelle."

"I see that." Noelle sighed. "I don't know. He's fine. He's nice, yes. But...*Bitsy*? Please."

"So they have nicknames," Angie said. "Once, about a hundred years ago, Craig called me 'Angel Dust.' I thought it was cute until I found out it was a name for a really bad drug in the eighties."

"But...overalls." Noelle rolled her eyes.

"Who cares what she wears?"

"It's a sign of how much she's changed, and she was perfect and didn't need to change."

"She's still perfect and if you ask me, the woman rocks a pair of overalls."

"That she does," Noelle agreed.

"Maybe you should try a pair," Angie teased. "With some of your red-bottom shoes?"

Noelle tried to curl her lip but laughed instead. "Farm chic. I could start a whole new trend in New York." She shook her head and gave her hand a flick. "I have to work, Ange."

"Seriously? You don't want to poke around the cabin and see all the changes? Aunt Elizabeth went off with Sonny to handle something on his farm, and the kids are on bear watch. We have the place to ourselves. I'm sure we could scare up an Irish coffee."

Noelle smiled. "Later, I promise. Now, I have twenty zillion emails to return, a client that's screaming at me, and Lucinda, the boss lady, is demanding a spreadsheet on last month's deals, which I am trying to create."

"And you like this job why?"

She lifted her hand, rubbing her fingers together in the universal gesture for cash.

"There's more to life than money," Angie said, a little disappointed and sad for her sister.

"Well, it's my career, which is my identity." She squinted at the screen. "And she wants the spreadsheet *yesterday*."

"In other words, leave." Angie laughed and stood, getting the message.

"Yes, only said with love and politeness."

Angie blew her a kiss and headed downstairs to find Eve at the picture window, staring out at the rolling Blue Ridge Mountains, a phone in her hand.

"Did you reach David?" Angie asked.

She turned, looking a little startled. "Oh, no. He's in surgery. I left a message. How's Noelle?"

"Pouting," Angie said. "I fear Aunt 'Bitsy' has toppled from the pedestal Noelle placed her on and our sweet sister is struggling under the weight of change."

"She's not a fan of anything new and different," Eve mused.

"How about you? What do you make of the all-new Aunt...Bitsy?"

Eve smiled. "Well, I think it's incredible, but I'm a

romantic at heart. Everyone deserves love, don't you think?"

"Absolutely," Angie agreed, tempted to elaborate about how her current state of love was in bad shape. But the cabin was comforting and bathed in late afternoon sun and she simply didn't feel like any more emotional revelations. "What are you going to do now?" she asked.

Eve bit back a playful smile. "Honestly? I was thinking about surprising Aunt Elizabeth by diving into the decorations in the attic. At least pulling out what we have and making our Christmas game plan."

"Maybe that's where I've gone wrong in my life. I've never had a Christmas game plan." Angie's mind flashed to Craig and Brooke back in California, and her heart ached when she realized she hadn't received even a thumbs-up to her text that said she'd landed safely in Asheville. The pang of hurt was harsh, but she dismissed it with a smile.

"No Christmas game plan?" Eve feigned shock. "How do you get through the holidays, my dear?"

"Poorly. Want to up my game...plan?"

"Let's go," Eve said, reaching for her hand. "This will be a master class in Christmas décor, you know. Dressing this place up like we used to is going to be no small project, but I'm eager to get my hands on those boxes. It's been so many years."

Angie took a step, then paused, searching her sister's face. "We can do this, right? Go headlong into memories of Mom and Dad? We're ready?"

"I am," Eve said. "Especially if we're together."

Just as they turned to go upstairs, they caught sight of the three boys—and one dog—outside, running up the road toward the house.

"Hang on a sec," Eve said, walking to the front door to open it. "Hey, guys. Aunt Angie and I are going up to the attic to start gathering Christmas decorations. Anyone want to help?"

"I will!" Bradley said.

"Not me." Sawyer fell to his knees and wrapped his arms around the dog's neck. "I'm staying outside forever with Lucky!"

"He's not dramatic or anything," Angie joked.

"And yet James is the one in plays."

"I'll stay with him, Mom," James said. "And don't worry. We haven't seen any bears."

"Yet!" Sawyer added, holding up a hopeful finger.

Bradley was already marching up the steps, kicking some snowy mud off his shoes, which he untied, took off, and neatly placed by the door.

"This place is so cool," he said, his cheeks bright from exertion. "But I want to see the attic, too."

Eve wrapped her arm around his narrow shoulders. "My little buddy."

Another pang of sadness hit Angie as they walked upstairs, thinking of how Brooke used to be *her* little buddy. These days, her daughter couldn't so much as glance her way or send her a text or, heaven forbid, spend the holidays with her.

But this was not the time to dwell. Life in California would figure itself out after Christmas, or at least that's what she was determined to tell herself. Today—this month—she would stay mired in the beauty and hominess of these mountains, happily ignoring her problems for as long as she could. Here, she was with family who loved her.

Down a hall from the boys' loft, they came to a small door, about as tall as Bradley.

"Whoa, cool! It's like a Harry Potter door!" Bradley grabbed the handle on the tiny hatch that led to the attic, but didn't open it, looking warily at his mother. "Any ghosts, goblins, dark wizards, or otherwise terrifying creatures on the other side?"

"Spiders," Angie said. "And I have a crippling fear."

"The one thing I'm not afraid of," Bradley said with manly courage. "In I go."

Angie and Eve shared a look and a quick laugh as he opened the door, and ducked down into the small opening, which was essentially an undersized hall leading to the actual attic.

Eve reached in and flipped a switch, bathing the small area in fluorescent light.

"Mom! Aunt Angie! Come on in!"

They followed him past the rough-hewn walls of the narrow opening.

"It's all coming back to me," Eve said.

"The creeps. That's what's coming back to me," Angie cracked.

Taking each other's hands with far less courage than little Bradley, they wiggled through the entry and then stepped into the real attic, a long, vaulted-ceiling area that smelled like dust and wood and probably some dead spiders. Hopefully dead.

A small, diamond-shaped window at the very end faced the front yard and allowed in enough light to show rows of wooden shelving, piles of boxes, an assortment of lamps, furniture, books, and pictures. Every square inch seemed to be piled with generations of memories and storage and history, some preserved, some just abandoned to be dealt with some other day.

"This is so neat!" Bradley climbed over a stack of bins, pulling out one of Eve's father's old vinyl records, turning the jacket over like it was utterly mystical to him. "What's the Fifth Dimension?"

Angie and Eve shared a look, both snorting a laugh.

"How many times did he make us listen to *The Age of Aquarius?*" Eve asked.

"So, so many," Angie replied with a sad smile, looking around and running her finger across a layer of dust that covered the boxes. "This is kind of amazing, Eve. Lots of history. Aunt Elizabeth must have moved some of Mom and Dad's things here after we went to college."

"Yeah." Eve sighed wistfully. "So many little pieces of them are in here."

"Right?" Angie picked up an old velvet hat box off of a shelf. "This couldn't have been Mom's."

"Maybe Granny Jane," Eve suggested. "But it could go back even further than that. This place was originally built by...Mom's grandmother. That would be our great-grandmother. That would be your great-great-granny, Bradley."

He drew back. "I have one of those?"

Angie tipped her head, a new kind of sadness hitting her. "You know, Mom was the keeper of all that information. Aunt Elizabeth never seemed to care that much about family history or genealogy."

"She might now, with this new change."

"Maybe," Angie conceded. "I sure could become obsessed with it. I imagine there's a treasure trove of Whitaker history up here. What was Mom's mother's maiden name?"

"Ummm...I'm not sure. I'd know it if I heard it. And while I respect that search, we're here for Christmas, so let's find the decorations." She turned and scanned the area. "Where the heck are they, though? I know Mom and Dad used to keep this majorly organized."

"Are you kidding?" Angie rolled her eyes. "Those Christmas decorations were like their fourth child. I'm sure they're all neatly tucked away and labeled with love."

"Here's a bear for Soy Sauce," Bradley joked, picking up a stuffed brown bear that looked well loved and very, very old.

"Ah, look at that." Eve took it gently from him.

"Was it yours, Mommy?" he asked.

She shook her head and showed it to Angie. "Not ours, and from the looks of it? Maybe not even our mother's or Aunt Elizabeth's. This is old."

"But sweet." Angie took it from her, admiring the craftsmanship of a toy that was clearly sewn by hand a long, long time ago. Black beady eyes stared at her and the fur was worn in places. "Probably worth something in an antique shop."

"Sawyer loves stuffed animals," Bradley said, losing interest and moving to the next box.

"You should give it to Sawyer for Christmas, Eve," Angie said. "This thing needs to be loved and it's part of the family."

"That's a great idea," she agreed, setting it aside.

Bradley popped his head out from behind a pile of plastic storage bins with the lids duct-taped on. "These say 'Christmas Stuff' on them!"

"Perfect!" Eve and Angie walked over to the bins that Bradley was examining, but were stunned to find the top one empty.

"Huh." Angie frowned as they pulled the lid off another, revealing nothing but some scraps of tissue paper and stray pine needles. "Where are they?"

"These are all empty," Bradley declared, searching the other bins one by one. "Most of them, anyway. This one has some lights, but that's it."

"That's weird." Eve leaned back against the wooden wall, toying with a string of lights in her hands. "Well, it was Christmas when the accident happened, so...Mom and Dad weren't here to take everything down."

"Oh, that's right." Angie closed her eyes and mentally drifted back to that, the worst day of her life. Of all their lives. "You're right. I mean, we stayed here that night with Aunt Elizabeth, then she took us straight home to Raleigh the next day. Gosh, I barely remember it, but none of us took the stuff down."

"Whoever did it..." Eve pointed to the empty bin. "Didn't follow the system."

"They've got to be up here somewhere!" Bradley insisted, his determined spirit lightening the mood.

"You're right, buddy." Eve brushed off the front of her jeans. "Let's keep looking."

The search continued, through cardboard boxes, bins, trunks, everything they could take apart. One by one, they began to find a few wintry and holiday things.

Angie discovered wreaths shoved in a bin full of the girls' elementary school yearbooks. Eve found candlesticks and garlands underneath a pile of winter clothes. Bradley dug up thousands of string lights from various hiding places, and even found their parents' precious Nativity scene.

After a thorough search, they seemed to have all the Christmas decorations accounted for, except for one critical piece: the ornaments.

The hundreds of cherished memories, horrendous elementary school art, darling childhood pictures, and handmade, heartfelt pieces. Each ornament had been a meaningful little token of the love and joy that had permeated their family. The ornaments weren't fancy or expensive or aesthetically pleasing, and their tree certainly didn't look like it came from the pages of the *Southern Living* Christmas edition.

But all of them were precious relics, treasured creations that Angie, Eve, and Noelle had made or bought as children, and included one for each daughter that their mother had picked every year. A ballet dancer for the year Noelle took dance, or a set of flipflops to remember a beach vacation. Angie could still see the little guitar that played music to commemorate the year she took lessons, certain she'd be the next Shania Twain.

And suddenly, an unexpected sadness washed over her. A deep grief for all the ornaments that *never* happened. The diplomas for graduation years or keys for when they got their licenses, the commemorations of their weddings, or the births of each of Jackie Chambers' grandchildren.

Well, they didn't exist, she thought, swallowing a lump that formed in her throat.

But the old ones did exist, and Angie was determined to find them. Those ornaments painted a picture of a family that had been whole and happy for fifteen years, and they meant everything to her.

"We'll find them," Eve asserted, no doubt sharing Angie's determination. "And, you know what? I'll ask David to bring a box of ours, so we have some from more recent Christmases."

Angie nodded, wishing she could ask Craig to do the same, but knowing that was a pipe dream that would never happen.

"Yeah, we'll find them." Bradley lifted his chin and mimicked his mother's confident certainty. "What's under those blankets?"

He pointed to the back corner of the attic where piles of wool throws covered a rectangular box pushed under a deep shelf.

On a prayer, Angie pulled off the layer of blankets,

coughing a bit as she waved off the cloud of dust that puffed out in front of her. Underneath the blankets was a big, metal trunk, latched shut.

"What's this?" she asked, waving her sister over.

Eve frowned, crouching down to get a better look before unclipping the two big latches. "Let's open it."

"Whoa, it's heavy," Angie said as she tried to lift the lid.

"Let me reach in." Bradley stuck his much smaller hand in the tiny opening, feeling around.

"You are a braver man than I am," Angie joked.

"Oh, oh!" He slipped his arm out, holding a red and white plastic candy cane with a hook hanging off it. "Ta-da!"

"Ornaments!" they all exclaimed, sharing a victorious high-five.

It took some maneuvering to drag the trunk out from under a shelf, but they finally got it free and open. Bradley dove right into the ornaments, instantly occupied and captivated by the old art projects and memories.

Eve sat down next to him, showing him the snowman that Aunt Noelle made in first grade, and Bradley giggled.

As Angie walked behind the trunk to get on the other side, something on the floor caught her eye.

A corner of paper, sticking up between some noticeably uneven floorboards that had been exposed when they moved the trunk.

"What's this?" she asked, crouching down and leaning over to study the yellowed flap.

"Not sure," Eve answered, distracted by the Santa she was dangling in front of her son.

Angie took the old, yellowed paper between her fingertips, feeling crispy edges and a dusty surface. She pushed the floorboard next to it, jiggling it. Was it loose?

Yes, it was, and it detached with no more than a flick of her finger, lifting up completely.

"What the heck..." Angie whispered as she peered into a sizeable hole built into the floor. Inside, she saw a metal case with a handle and a silver latch, partially covered by a yellowed newspaper. "Eve, look at this."

"What is it?" Eve scooted over and craned her neck to see the floorboards. "Oh, my gosh, a secret space! What's in there?"

Blowing out a steadying breath, Angie gingerly lifted a corner of the old newspaper, squinting at the faded headline.

Infant saved in Biltmore Estate Fire

"What's the date?" Eve asked.

"January 10, 1924. That's just about a hundred years ago!" Chills blossomed over Angie's arms as she angled the newspaper toward the light, trying to make out the faded type of the lead story. "'A small fire in one of the guest rooms at the Biltmore House where distant relatives to the Vanderbilt family were staying nearly cost the life of a four-month-old infant. Baby Claudia Winchester, daughter of Mr. and Mrs. Keegan Winchester, was asleep in the Damask Room on the second floor when the canopy caught fire from a candle.

Despite flames and smoke, a parlor maid by the name of Angelica Benson risked her life—"

"That's it!" Eve exclaimed. "Benson! That's Granny Jane's maiden name!"

"You're right," Angie said, as the chills seemed to multiply. "And listen to this: 'Angelica Benson risked her life to save the baby. Both escaped with modest injuries, although the cost of the repairs to the bedrooms will be in the many thousands.'"

Angie's jaw dropped as it all sank in and she looked from Eve to the paper and back to Eve again. "Angelica is our great-grandmother! Granny Jane's mother. When did she die?"

"Long before we were born. In the 1970s, I think."

"Angelica Benson," Angie whispered. "Do you think I was named after her?"

"Maybe. Dad always said he wanted to name the third Christmas triplet Holly, but Mom let her mother pick the name and maybe she named you after *her* mother, but kept the Christmas theme by shortening it to Angel for Angelica—who was a hero!"

Angie made a little squeal of happiness. "How incredibly cool is that?"

"Read the rest," Eve urged. "I want to hear what happened."

Eve skimmed through the article, zeroing in on a quote from Louise Winchester. "'My heart has been saved by Mrs. Benson. Without her valor, the only thing that has ever mattered to me—my infant daughter—would surely have perished. She will be well compensated. Mrs. Benson is married to Garland Benson, who is a footman at the estate.' And that must be our great-grandfather!"

"What's a footman?" Bradley asked, coming closer. "And is an estate a palace?"

Angie laughed. "Well, my entire knowledge of this era of history comes from binging *Downton Abbey*, so if that was correct, they served dinner and such. The Biltmore Estate is a very famous American castle right in Asheville where tourists march through to gaze at hundred-year-old furniture."

"That sounds boring," Bradley said with an eye roll.

"Not to me," Angie said. "It sounds amazing." With reverence, she gently set the newspaper on a cleared section of the floor. "Let's see what else is in here."

Reaching in, she lifted the metal box, which was sizeable and heavy. With a grunt, she pulled it out and placed it on the floor.

"I'll start carrying this stuff down, okay, Mom?" Bradley called.

"Okay, but can you take this bear and hide it under my bed so Sawyer doesn't see it?" She handed him the stuffed animal. "And then get your brothers, 'cause we'll need extra arms."

"Okay."

When he left, Eve leaned closer to the box. "Is it locked?"

"No." She lifted the latch and opened the thin metal box, sucking in a soft breath at the sight of what felt like pirate treasure. In truth, it was some clothes, a delicate brooch in the shape of a flower, and a tin with a picture of Buckingham Palace painted on it. There was also a thick old photo of a woman holding a baby. On the back, someone had written, "Baby Claudia with her angel, Angelica."

"Oh, that's her," Angie said, blinking at the image of the woman.

"There's another newspaper," Eve said, pointing at the last thing in the case.

Angie lifted it, the paper folded to a feature article announcing that Louise and Keegan Winchester had gifted the Bensons with six acres of land on Copper Creek Mountain and a substantial sum to fund the building of a cottage where they would live after retiring from their service at the Biltmore Estate.

"That's this cabin!" Angie said.

"All because your namesake walked through fire to save a baby!" Eve exclaimed.

Angie let out a long, slow breath of pure enchantment. "I have to know more about her. About them, and what they did for the Vanderbilt family. Do you think Aunt Elizabeth knows?"

"Maybe. This cabin was built in the late 1920s, I think, and Mom and Aunt Elizabeth were born in Raleigh and that was the late 1950s. But Aunt Elizabeth might know something."

"Granny Jane used to always say her mother 'earned' this cabin," Angie said as the memory floated back. "This must be what she meant." Angie tenderly smoothed the newspaper, then picked up the picture. "Look at Angelica! She's beautiful."

"She looks like Mom, don't you think?"

"A little, in the eyes," Angie agreed.

They studied the black and white photograph of the woman, who had long, dark hair, and delicate bone structure.

"This is just incredible," Angie whispered. "This woman is our great-grandmother, and she worked at the Biltmore House and she built this cabin on land they gave her and...she has my name."

Eve nodded in equal amazement. "I can't wait to ask Aunt Elizabeth what she knows about this. It's such cool family folklore."

Angie leaned back, toying with the newspaper between her fingertips. "The Biltmore Estate is close. I know we toured it once with Mom and Dad."

Eve shrugged. "Twenty or twenty-five minutes, I think."

Angie felt a smile pull as an unfamiliar burn ignited inside her. "I have to know more. I want to know more about this woman, her job, and that fire, and...everything. It's weird, but I feel such a connection to her."

"You do share her name."

"I do," she admitted. "You know, I think I'm going to go to the Biltmore Estate while we're here and see what I can find out."

"Good luck with that," Eve said wryly. "You have to book tickets months in advance to see their epic Christmas display. Every tourist within fifty miles of

Asheville goes there in December. I think they have more than a hundred Christmas trees."

Angie shrugged, carefully gathering up the items and returning them to the metal box she would be taking down to her room.

"Well, I'll call, then. They may want some of this memorabilia, and I'd like information."

"Who needs strong men?" Sawyer called. "'Cause we're here!"

They smiled at each other and turned from their find to haul decorations all the way down to the living room.

The entire time, Angie couldn't stop thinking about her great-grandmother. It was strange, but for the first time in what felt like forever, her heart was light with hope and excitement about something new.

Chapter Seven

Noelle

"STANFORD? Stanford, can you hear me? You're breaking up." Noelle pressed her iPhone to her ear, hopping off the twin bed and pacing the bedroom.

"I'm sorry...Noelle...that will not...call him..." The broken voice of Stanford Monmouth, the owner of Monmouth Art Gallery in Miami, made her nearly moan with frustration. What was he saying?

"Didn't quite get that, Stanford, but I do have a buyer for that Yarrow McFarland piece, if you can send me... Stanford? Are you there? Can you hear me?"

Nothing.

Dang it, she'd been trying to sell that Yarrow painting for months, and Stanford had been so close to accepting the offer.

She couldn't lose this deal!

Clutching the phone, she rushed down the stairs and shot out the front door in a desperate attempt to find phone service. She stabbed the screen to call him back, joyous when he answered.

"Noelle...got that...but I can't...."

She dropped her head back with a whimper at the broken words. "I'm in the mountains right now with a lousy signal. Can you hear me? Can you..."

Again, nothing.

"Oh, come on," she grumbled, staring at the phone like it could magically connect to real service and let her close a deal that could get her well past this month's quota.

She inhaled, the numbers on that spreadsheet dancing in her head. Well past quota. In fact, at this rate, she'd make...

She suddenly forgot the money as the clean, cold air filled her lungs, the scent of pine and wintry earth dragging her back to the moment.

There's more to life than money...

The echo of Angie's pronouncement rang in her ears, loud and clear and...true.

Easy for Angie to say—she was married, had a daughter, and probably had a very wonderful life in California despite not seeming too pleased with it at the moment. Eve, too, had all the things that allegedly gave an-almost-forty-year-old woman joy. And now, even Aunt Elizabeth had flipped the books on independent women everywhere and fallen in love.

Noelle closed her eyes, letting that last one hit the hardest. As soon as she stopped working, she started thinking about it again. She knew she should be happy for her aunt, but she felt something else she didn't understand and couldn't name.

She glanced at her phone, which sported a distinct

lack of bars and service, and shoved it in her pocket, heading back into the house. She'd heard Angie and Eve go up into the attic a while ago and she probably should see what they were up to, but all she wanted to do was... be alone.

Inside, she snagged a heavy wool sweater from a hook, stuck her feet in a pair of beat-up hiking boots that looked like they had Bitsy written all over them, and headed out to breathe more of that fresh Carolina air.

She followed the path she'd known as a little girl, along the driveway to Creekside Road, turning at the red mailbox, then heading down a hill, the rocky path feeling weirdly familiar.

Noelle shut her eyes, took a lungful of delicious oxygen, and attempted to gather her thoughts. It was beautiful here—rural and rustic and certainly not her typical cup of tea, but it was impossible to deny the homey nostalgia and connection she felt to this place.

But the beauty of the Blue Ridge Mountains and the childhood memories of the cabin were one thing. Aunt Elizabeth as the latest contestant on *The Farmer Wants a Wife*? That was a whole different can of worms.

Why was it so upsetting to her, Noelle wondered. Why did this feel like a disappointment or betrayal? She should be jumping for joy but all she felt was...

Good heavens. Was she *jealous* of Aunt Elizabeth? How small. How shameful. No. She didn't want a man who'd change her the way Old MacDonald—okay, McPherson—had changed Elizabeth Whitaker. She didn't want any man intruding on her solitude and privacy or dipping into her healthy bank account and...

There's more to life than money...

"Oh, hush up, Angel Chambers Messina," Noelle whispered to herself as she speed-walked down the road, her feet crunching over dead leaves and small piles of snow that had gathered in the shadowy places of the mountain.

Pausing on the side, she looked out as the sun dipped closer to the distant mountains, gilding the horizon. This was so different from the world where she lived. Part of her loved it so much she wanted to cry, and part of her—the part that felt safe when she was surrounded by cement and strangers and cabs—just wanted to run home and be...lonely.

Was she really that lonely? Was that what caused the low-grade ache she sometimes felt, the sensation she always attributed to stress or work or an old, old sadness? Was loneliness what caused her to feel like she was always searching for something, the next promotion, the next deal, the next new purchase?

She sighed deeply, not sure how she'd gone from a frustrating work call to questioning her very reason for living. Before she knew it, she'd hiked around the curve of Creekside Road, down nearly to the next property.

She was about to turn around and head back up to the house when a white pickup truck rumbled closer and she stepped off to the bramble on the side of the road, realizing it was the first vehicle she'd seen on this whole walk.

Was it Sonny? In a different truck, perhaps? He probably owned several, in addition to a few tractors and stock in John Deere.

The truck stopped as it reached her, and the window slid down to reveal a man at the wheel. That was definitely not Sonny McPherson, even though he wore the obligatory ballcap and flannel shirt.

This man was around forty or so, his strong jaw dark with a day-old beard, a few strands of chestnut hair visible and brushing the collar of his shirt. He pinned gray-blue eyes on her with a look of curiosity and interest.

"Ma'am?"

She cocked her head, unsure what to say as she studied his features, which seemed as vaguely familiar as this road and these hills. A Carolina man, she supposed, with an air of country and courtesy that probably melted every woman for miles.

She was too cold to melt, though, so she crossed her arms over her chest. "I'm not lost," she announced, expecting that's why he stopped. "I'm just out for a walk."

"Oh, that's good, because I'm looking for someone who might be lost and..." He narrowed his eyes as he studied her, a slight smile revealing straight teeth that, like the subtle drawl, suddenly seemed as familiar as a song from her childhood. "Suppose I should tell you my name so you know I'm not a kidnapper. I'm Jace Fleming and my—"

"Jace?" She gasped the name, the familiarity flipping to a crystal-clear image of a boy she hadn't seen in twenty-five years, now...a man in a flannel shirt and a ballcap. "Are you kidding me?"

"Do I...do I..." His jaw dropped. "Well, as I live and breathe. If it isn't Noelle Chambers come back to Copper Creek."

For a second, she couldn't speak, taking in the sight of an old friend, a treasured memory, and a full-blown crush.

"Jace," she whispered. "I had no idea you still lived here."

He looked dumbstruck, too, staring at her like she... well, like she was the most beautiful thing he'd ever seen. He'd always looked at her that way. It had been the headiest feeling at fifteen...and it wasn't bad at thirty-nine, either.

"I can't believe it." He flipped open the door and stepped out like nothing could keep him from getting closer. "How are you?" He reached out his arms and she didn't even think, but stepped right into the hug he offered, letting out a musical laugh of happiness and surprise.

"I'm good, I'm good." Drawing back, they separated and stared for another few seconds, and she had no doubt he was remembering the summers and Christmases all those years ago.

They'd started out as childhood friends who spent time fishing or hiking or running around with her dog, Rascal. At thirteen, they held hands when Angie and Eve weren't around, sharing secrets about their lives and experiences at school.

The summer she was fourteen, they confessed how much they liked each other, and that last time, that last Christmas when she turned fifteen, he'd asked her to be his girlfriend, even though they lived in different towns.

That moment had been down by the wide part of the creek, by the old shack. She'd told him she'd meet him there the next day and tell him yes or no...but there had never been a next day. Her parents had been killed that night.

"You look great," Jace said with a smile, a glint of warm admiration in his gaze. "You haven't changed. I mean, you have the same smile and...those big brown eyes." He shook his head with a self-conscious laugh. "Always had a weakness for brunettes after you."

She laughed, trying to control the jitters that came so naturally around him. "You look great," she said. "Like a..." *Like a dream in a flannel shirt*, she thought, but managed to just smile. "Like a real Carolina man."

"That I am," he said. "But I have left this mountain, believe it or not."

"Are you just back for the holidays?" she asked.

"Oh, no, no. I live here now. I went to Chapel Hill for vet school and came back to start my own practice."

"Oh, that makes perfect sense," she exclaimed as her heart tugged. "You always worried about Rascal when we hiked. And I seem to recall a turtle rescue at the creek and the need to leave food for the deer."

He laughed. "Guilty as charged. I actually do large animals. You know, all the farms around here."

Well, she knew a farmer as of today. "That's wonderful. I'm so happy for you."

"And you..." Jace gestured at her, his brows lifting. "Wait, I heard this. You live in New York, right? Doing what your aunt used to do for...something with art."

"How do you know?"

"I know your aunt through Sonny. I asked her how you were doing."

He'd asked about her? For some reason, that gave her a little shiver of delight. "Well, all that's true."

"Never expected to see you back here, though," he said.

"Blame Elizabeth Whitaker. She's brought us all back here for the whole month of December to have a proper Asheville Christmas. I never thought that would happen after..."

His whole expression grew serious. "Gosh, Noelle, I know this is a whole lot of years too late, but I'm sorry about your parents. I never got a chance to tell you."

"Thank you," she said. "I'm sorry I left without an explanation."

"You didn't need one and I should have called you or gone to see you in Raleigh, but I...I still didn't have a license and even if I had, I didn't know what to say." He gave a tight smile. "I was as awkward then as I am now."

He wasn't the least bit awkward, then or now. But he *had* been about three inches shorter and skinny. Now he broke six feet and looked like he could lift those large animals he cared for.

"It's fine," she assured him. "I wasn't good company back in those days."

He nodded slowly, still studying her face like an appraiser looking at a piece of art, itching to bid. "So, all of December, huh? That's...cool."

"It's...been interesting so far. We just met Sonny and found out he's won my aunt's heart."

"Oh, those two are like a couple of teenagers." He chuckled. "I guess I can say that from experience."

She felt some heat crawl from her chest to her face, and tried to remember the last time a man made her feel a little off-kilter like this. Probably this man, on this mountain.

"But, hey, he's a great guy," he said quickly, as if he suddenly realized he was flirting. "I take care of all his animals, and the man's got some beautiful horses. You should take Jasper for a ride. He's a terrific horse."

"Oh, I don't...ride horses. And my Aunt Elizabeth?" She shook her head. "She didn't even like dogs when we were little. She was always complaining about Rascal leaving hair on her St. John Knits clothes."

He shrugged. "Don't know what that means, but Bitsy loves all the animals now."

"Bitsy?" Her eyes shuttered. "I can't believe she lets people call her that."

"I think she loves that name and, you know, people change."

She nodded, too happy to see him to delve into the subject.

"Noelle Chambers." He shook his head, laughing softly. "What a world."

She sucked in a breath and gave a tight smile. "Life is funny, isn't it?"

"It's never boring, that's for sure. I mean, I feel like—"

"Daddy! Daddy!"

Noelle whipped around to see a little girl, probably about the same age as Bradley, skipping up the road in dirty jeans and an oversized sweater, her arm outstretched with a leash leading a...no, that wasn't any kind of dog Noelle had ever seen. Was that a *goat*?

But she didn't take a minute to figure out what it was because...she'd called him Daddy.

Her heart sank instantly as the realization hit her. *This little country nymph is his daughter, and he is, of course, married.* Why wouldn't he be? He was handsome, sweet, kind, and just as pure as he was at fifteen.

He probably had a wife at home who was country and wholesome, churning butter and making babies. Just as happy as two people could be.

"There you are, Cassie!" He lunged toward her, those long arms out. "I've been driving all over creation trying to find you, girl."

As she got closer, Noelle noticed her hair was in uneven pigtails with mismatched bows, her smile revealing a space between brand-new teeth. "Sorry, Daddy. Sprinkles needed extra walking time today. She was running all over the place and had to just walk all that energy off!"

She punctuated the announcement by throwing one hand dramatically in the air.

"Not a mile from home," Jace said, putting a hand on the little girl's shoulder and ushering her closer. "Noelle, this is my daughter, Cassie, and her wayward goat, Sprinkles. Honey, this is Noelle Chambers..." He glanced at her with a slight frown. "Unless...is that still your last name?"

She nodded, feeling a faint glimmer of hope that he was asking if she was married. Not that she hoped for anything with Jace, but...

"Hello," Cassie said, coming closer. "She's just high energy, not wayward, whatever that means."

Noelle laughed and looked at the gray and white animal with pointy ears and big eyes. "I did goat yoga once," she said. "They were pretty chill creatures."

"Goat yoga?" Cassie's eyes, the same silvery blue as her father's, widened. "What is that and when can we?"

Jace cracked up and looked skyward with fake exasperation. "Warning, she's not shy. She got that from her mother."

Noelle tamped down the completely unwelcome disappointment in Jace's very much not singleness. Of course he was happily married with an adorable child and a goat named Sprinkles.

"Well, shyness is highly overrated, Cassie," she said, smiling at the child. "And, to be honest, so is goat yoga."

Cassie studied her...hard. "You're pretty," she finally said.

"Told ya," Jace muttered. "No filter."

Noelle smiled at her. "You're quite pretty yourself."

"Those are fancy jeans."

"Well, I don't have a lot of outdoor clothes, that's all. I spend most of my time in offices."

Cassie scrunched up her face, her tiny button nose wrinkling. "What offices?"

"Not here," Noelle explained. "In New York. That's where I live."

"Oh." Her eyes widened, and she stretched an arm up way over her head. "With the real tall buildings. You live in one of those?"

Noelle glanced at Jace, then back at his little girl. "I do. On the seventeenth floor."

"Wow! That's cool. But I like it on the ground with the animals because they need walks," Cassie announced, nodding toward Sprinkles. "So it's my job to take them, rain or shine."

Jace gave an endearing shrug. "The animal thing...it's hereditary."

"Do you have a farm, too?" she asked, weirdly interested in how he lived...with his wife and daughter and goat.

"Not technically, but my vet practice is on my ranch, and we keep some animals for overnight visits and boarding. We've usually got a few at any given time, and Cassie here is the official walker."

"They like me the best," Cassie told her.

"I don't doubt that," Noelle said. "I've never seen a goat on a leash before, but Sprinkles looks like she's never been happier."

The goat bleated as if to confirm that, inching closer to Cassie.

"All right, we better get going," Jace said after a beat, going to the back of the truck to open up the tailgate and gesture for her, and the goat, to climb in. "You, young lady, need to get home and cleaned up for your play rehearsal."

"A play?" Noelle asked. "That sounds like fun. Do you have a big part?"

"I'm the angel at the birth of baby Jesus," Cassie told her solemnly as she shoved Sprinkles in the truck bed and followed. "The only part more important is played by a baby doll covered in manger hay."

Noelle looked at Jace, wondering if this precious child could even be real. How did he get so lucky?

He shrugged as he got back behind the wheel, as if he knew exactly what she was thinking. "Can't argue with that logic," he said.

For a moment, she let herself imagine that play, that angel, that doll in a manger. She pictured Jace with his flannel shirt and handsome face, holding his wife's hand as they beamed with pride at their precious angel.

The whole thing just made her feel...lonely. *Again.*

Jace smiled as he closed the door, his gaze lingering on Noelle, the twenty-five years of distance and silence hanging in the air between them. "It was really great to see you again, Noelle."

"It was great to see you, too. And lovely to meet you, Cassie." She smiled at the little girl who'd settled with both arms around Sprinkles.

"I'm sure I'll catch you around," Jace said as he shifted the truck into gear to drive off. "I'm always helping out Sonny and Bitsy with something or other."

"I'll...look forward to that," she said. "I'd love to meet your wife."

Instantly, his expression changed from warmth to something much more bittersweet. "Uh, no, she..." He turned toward her and lowered his voice. "She passed away when Cassie was just a toddler. We lost her to cancer."

"Oh." She pressed her fingertips to her mouth, suddenly awash in a swirling cocktail of sympathy and surprise and no small amount of shame for the thread of jealousy she'd felt toward the woman. "I'm so sorry, Jace."

He nodded a silent thanks. "Cass and I are a good team. And, you know, Sprinkles."

She smiled at that, not having a clue what to say. "Well, that's...wow. You've been through a lot."

"We both have," he reminded her. "And now...off to play practice. Make sure she knows how to say her lines."

"I know them, Daddy! 'Glory to God in the highest! Peace to His people on Earth! For tonight a child is born—'"

He cut her off by turning the engine on noisily.

Chuckling, Noelle waved again. "Bye, Cassie! So nice to meet you!"

"See ya around, Miss Noelle," Jace said with a parting wink that curled poor Noelle's toes in her dirty old boots.

"Bye, Jace."

She stood for a moment on the side of the road, watching his truck disappear around the next corner, a little breathless from the unexpected encounter.

As she headed home, thinking about Jace and his adorable daughter and country vet life, the echo of her sister's words haunted her.

There's more to life than money...

She bet Jace Fleming knew that, and learned it the hardest possible way.

Chapter Eight

Eve

WAKING up at the cabin sent a flood of bittersweet familiarity washing over Eve as she tucked herself underneath the handmade patchwork quilt. It was early, only a little after six, but the light was slipping through the shutters. Rising, she peeked outside and saw delicate flurries of snow dancing through the frosty morning air.

Time for coffee, peace, and morning quiet. Sliding her feet into fuzzy slippers, she wrapped a warm robe around her and tied it as she tiptoed through the hallway and down the stairs.

A few minutes later, she held a steaming mug of coffee and stepped out to the quiet of the glass-enclosed all-season porch to enjoy the morning view. Aunt Elizabeth had done plenty of work in this sunroom, adding screens to several of the windows, which probably made it lovely in the summer, too.

The blankets they'd tucked around them late last night after the boys had gone to bed were still strewn over the furniture, reminding her of the hours she'd shared with her sisters and Aunt Elizabeth.

Sonny had brought them the most insanely delicious fried chicken from Rocky's, which they'd all enjoyed family style. When he left and the boys had gone up to fall into bed after a day of mountain play, the four ladies had enjoyed Irish coffee and conversation.

Aunt Elizabeth shared what she knew—which was not much—about her grandmother, Angelica Benson, who had become Angie's obsession. And when Noelle told them about meeting her teenage crush, they also learned more about Jace, the widower veterinarian who, according to Noelle, had grown up "quite nicely."

It had been a dream of an evening, lasting late enough that everyone still slept, so Eve knew it was a perfect time to call David. She'd only been able to exchange brief texts yesterday, so she hadn't yet told him all the news.

She settled in and clicked his name on her phone screen, holding her breath as it rang a couple of times.

"Hi, sweetie!" David answered with that note that said he was always glad when she called, filling her with gratitude.

"Hey, I caught you," she said on a happy sigh.

"You called at the perfect time. I'm just on my way to the hospital. Long day ahead, but better now that I get to hear your voice. I wanted to call when I got in the car, but I figured you'd sleep in a bit longer."

"I woke with the sun," Eve said, watching the light change the tree colors and shift the panoramic Blue Ridge Mountains from dawn to daylight. "It's so gorgeous and peaceful here, David. And all this time with my sisters is such a blessing. Plus, the boys are already having the time of their lives."

"I'm so happy for you, Evie," David said, a hint of sadness in his tone, reminding her that he was feeling distant from them, too. "How is everyone? Is your Aunt Elizabeth okay? I know your text said her news was good, so can I assume you weren't summoned for an early reading of the will?"

She laughed at how far off they'd been. "Not unless you count the demise of her glamorous looks and clothes. Honey, she's a different and extremely content person who has met the loveliest man. Well, the second loveliest."

He chuckled at that. "A man, huh? Interesting. Who is this lucky boyfriend?"

She sipped her coffee and did her best to fill him in. "He's a local farmer named Sonny, if you can believe that. He owns a tractor and reads the Bible and has horses, cows, goats, and chickens. She's wearing overalls and has let her hair go gray, much to Noelle's consternation, but he's brought a light to my aunt that I didn't ever know was missing, but it was."

David was silent while he processed Eve's words, undoubtedly forming his own mental image of the world's most unlikely pairing.

"Well, there you have it." David laughed softly, and Eve could so clearly picture him shaking his head slowly, his handsome smile pulling at his freshly shaven cheeks. "Stranger than fiction, huh?"

"It really is. But she seems so...so *radiant*. I think it's wonderful that she's found true love and finally wants to settle down after all those years of her precious independence, which is another thing baffling Noelle."

"That's because she's always tried to be a younger version of Elizabeth," he said. "She'll get used to the idea. You have, but then, you are a hopeless romantic who loves love."

"That's a fact." She took another sip. "I really hope Noelle lets go of this grudge, though. Why wouldn't she want her dearest aunt to be happy?"

"Because it shakes the very foundation of all she's built her life on," he said simply.

Deep inside, Eve knew that, but coming from her logical and wise husband, it actually made sense.

"I'll have to be gentler on her," she said. "As always, you give the best advice."

"Just the male perspective. Speaking of, how are the boys?"

"Outdoorsmen, one and all. The word on the street is that they are taking a four-mile hike today with 'Uncle' Sonny and his golden retriever, Lucky. James is analyzing why the mountain air is so healthy, Bradley wants to be sure they have safe hiking shoes, and Sawyer is looking to make friends with a bear."

He laughed heartily. "So much for schoolwork."

"It's a big fat field trip and I'm here for it." Eve leaned back against the cushion of the loveseat, wrapping her hands around her warm mug as she relished the love and companionship she heard in every word they exchanged. "It's good for me, too," she added. "Except I miss you."

"I miss you so much, Evie. Waking up in the morning to a big empty house is tough. It's quiet without Sawyer singing to his Pop-Tarts or James practicing Spanish."

"Or Bradley offering to clean the dishes, vacuum the floors, and solve world hunger while he's at it."

David snorted. "We've got some good ones, don't we?"

Eve sighed wistfully. "Beyond good. So, you're getting in Friday afternoon? I can't wait. We're unpacking all the old decorations, and there's so much to—"

"Oh, Eve. I thought I told you."

Eve felt her heart drop like a cement brick in her chest. "Told me what?"

"I can't get out there until Sunday. I'm so sorry. There's a group of med students coming in from Chapel Hill and I got committed to taking them on rounds and doing an impromptu neuroendoscopy on Saturday morning."

"Saturday?" she choked.

"The manufacturer of this scope is coming to town and asked for a special weekend event. I'm actually the first surgeon to use it in a real-world app, and I promised months ago but totally forgot. I have to do it because I'm the only one in my group trained on it. Remember the trip to Nashville I took?"

"Oh, of course." Eve swallowed the familiar lump of disappointment that rose in her throat, pushing it away as she squeezed her eyes shut and held the phone to her ear. "That's okay. Sunday is fine."

"I'm really sorry, Eve. If anyone else could step in, I wouldn't have—"

"I know, David. It's okay, really. You're saving lives and teaching med students. It's much more important than..." *Me. Our family.* "Hanging around in the mountains."

David groaned. "All I want to *do* is hang around in the mountains with you and the boys, believe me. But I don't have anything scheduled for Monday or Tuesday and my patient calendar is clear, so I should be able to stay at least a couple of days."

"Okay." Eve forced herself to take a deep breath and appreciate everything beautiful that she had in her life. "We'll need you to help us cut down the tree."

"Oh, boy. Couldn't miss that for anything. And I just pulled into the hospital for rounds, so I gotta run. I love you. Hug the boys for me and say hi to your sisters. Oh, and Aunt Elizabeth and her new beau."

Eve laughed. "Of course. I love you."

"I love you, too. Bye, honey."

The sudden silence hit her right in the gut as she sat holding the phone in one hand and a nearly empty coffee cup in the other.

"Need some company?" Angie's voice caught Eve's attention, and she turned to see her sister standing in the doorway with a coffee of her own.

"Morning, Ange." Eve scooted over on the loveseat,

patting the spot next to her and extending her blanket. "Please join me."

Angie sat down next to her, her honey-colored waves loosely knotted up in an effortless bun. She wore her black-rimmed glasses, and her natural face was dotted with freckles, her skin glowing in the sun.

But Eve could easily see the troubled sadness in her sister's eyes—that familiar melancholy that seemed to float around Angie sometimes, particularly when she talked about life in California.

"How are you, sweet sister of mine?" She placed a hand on Angie's knee. "You seem a little blue."

Angie shrugged, sipping her coffee and staring out at the view. "I'm all right."

Eve shot her a look, narrowing her gaze. "Come on, Ange. What's going on with you? You've been super quiet on this trip, except when we're talking about a woman who lived a hundred years ago."

Angie blew out a breath, fluttering some strands of hair. "I guess being here has brought my issues to the surface."

"Which are...?"

"It's not exactly a secret that I don't love California," she said simply.

California...or Craig? Eve kept the question to herself and nodded with understanding. "We've noticed."

"I've been there for more than four years and I'm still waiting for it to feel like home," she admitted. "Like, I'm waiting for even the tiniest glimmer of home, or belonging, or connection. But it feels cold and lonely and distant, like I'm living someone else's life and I don't belong there at all. I mean *at all.*"

Eve swallowed, processing her sister's confession. "I knew you weren't thrilled on the West Coast, but I didn't realize it was that bad."

"It's bad," she admitted. "And here? I know it sounds ridiculous because we haven't even been here a full twenty-four hours, but my soul is at peace. I feel like I could belong here, you know? And not just because I found my namesake's picture and backstory in the attic, I swear, although that helps. But this cabin and the family and our roots in these mountains and Asheville? I honestly ache for more of it."

"I totally get that," Eve said.

"And then comes the guilt," Angie added on a dry laugh. "Big, fat gobs of guilt."

"For being happy without your family?" Eve guessed.

Angie pointed at her. "Bingo. My family is three thousand miles away, I'm not spending the holidays with my own husband and daughter, and yet I'm happier here. Doesn't that make me horrible?" Her voice cracked. "I'm more excited about my poor dead great-grandmother than I can remember being about anything in years. Shouldn't I just want to go home?"

Eve placed her hand over her sister's and gave it a squeeze. "You're not horrible, Ange. You're miserable out there. It's natural that you'd find joy here, in the cabin and with your sisters."

Angie lifted a shoulder, clearly not convinced. "I should want to get on a plane and go back and be with my husband and daughter. But the sad truth is, I'm kind of relieved. Brooke barely talks to me and Craig is..." She cleared her throat glancing away. "So busy."

Well, Eve could certainly relate to that. "I know what that's like, believe me."

"No, you don't. David isn't anything like Craig."

Eve looked down at her empty mug, not entirely sure what to say. She had never been a huge fan of Craig Messina, the ambitious, slick, and a little-too-charming salesman who swept Angie off her feet her senior year in college. But they'd always been happy enough, or at least she thought they had.

"Have you talked to Craig about how unhappy you are in California? I mean, maybe he'd consider a transfer."

Angie gave a derisive snort, shifting the blanket over her legs and shaking her head. "He'd sooner jump off a cliff than leave his lofty position at Atlas Technologies."

"But if you told him how unhappy you are—deeply and truly—wouldn't he want to change that?"

Angie closed her eyes. "Not my husband. My needs are not paramount. In fact, he most likely doesn't think I *have* needs. All that matters is his epic Silicon Valley career and if I don't like California?" She shifted on the sofa. "He'd probably suggest I leave...and for a lot longer than a month."

Eve recoiled. "Is your marriage really that shaky?"

Angie turned to her, her grass-green eyes sad and misty, her mouth turned down. She parted her lips and took a breath to say something—a typical Angie, dismissive, sarcastic crack to shut down Eve's worry. But all that came out was a soft, tiny sob.

"Oh, no." Eve moved closer for a hug as her sister cried quietly, wiping away tears.

"It's bad. It's so, so bad. He's hardly ever home. We never spend any time together anymore. When he is in the house, he's got a glass of scotch in his hand and he's tucked away in the office until late at night. He goes on business trips to God knows where every other week, and..." She sucked in a ragged breath, breaking Eve's heart. "It's like I don't even know him anymore. And he doesn't know me. We're strangers, living in a strange house, with an ice-cold, distant daughter who'd rather spend Christmas with her boyfriend's family than with either one of us."

Eve's heart cracked at the pain in Angie's voice. "I had no idea," she whispered, keeping a comforting arm around her. "I mean, I figured you guys were having a rough patch living all the way out there, and I knew Brooke has been tough to handle lately, but this sounds like so much more than that."

"It is." Angie sniffled. "We were okay before this job. Then he traded family for work. It took over everything. It's his love, his life, his passion. He's got nothing left for me or Brooke, and he's turned into this shell of himself. He's short-tempered and preoccupied and I feel like he can't *stand* me."

Eve shuddered, unable to envision that kind of love-less marriage, horrified by the thought of her wonderful sister having to endure it. "You really think it's all because of work?"

Angie swallowed, shrugging as she set her coffee mug down on the end table. "That's what changed everything. This job, and California. We grew apart little by little, you know? At first, we stopped having dinner together every night. Then we stopped making time for dates. He stayed at the office later and later, and went on more and more business trips. Before I knew it, I was standing in my kitchen staring at a man I no longer recognize."

"I'm so sorry." Eve frowned, hurting for Angie, but unable to ignore her own nagging worry.

Was her marriage with David destined for the same kind of distance? It felt like he worked constantly, and they never really had quality time together.

"No, *I'm* sorry." Angie moaned. "How about a nice trauma dump to go with your coffee and sunrise?"

"Please. I'm so glad you finally opened up. I knew things were not perfect by the way you talked about it at Thanksgiving. But I really didn't know how far gone it was."

"Far. Very far gone." She wiped her fingers under her eyes to dry the tears, taking in a deep breath and straightening her shoulders. "But I still want to fix it, you know?"

"Of course," Eve said quickly. A diehard perfectionist with a crippling fear of failure, Eve Gallagher knew all too well what it was like to want to fix what was broken. "A therapist, a vacation, some time alone? What can you do?"

"He scoffs at any of those things, so I'm hoping this

time apart will bring some clarity and maybe we'll even really miss each other. Of course, I wanted him to come here with me, but that wasn't in the cards."

Eve winced, the absence of her own husband pressing on her shoulders, heavier than ever.

"I wish I had good advice for you, Ange. But I'm also sitting here husband-less." Worry prickled across her skin as she said the words out loud.

"Oh, Eve, come on." Angie elbowed her playfully. "David is a saint and he worships the ground you walk on. It's nothing like my situation."

Eve chewed her lip, thinking about that. On one hand, she'd heard the joy in his voice when she called... along with the news that he had to teach med students on a Saturday. "I try to make it look easy, but it's hard. He's always at work, too."

Angie nodded, wrapping an arm around Eve. "You and David are going to be perfectly fine. I didn't mean to scare you with my marriage horror story."

"And I didn't mean to make it about myself," Eve replied quickly. "I'm sorry."

"It's okay. I feel better getting it off my chest. I could only fake like everything was fine for so long before I cracked."

Eve swallowed, nodding. "I'm really glad you were honest with me. That's what we're here for, Angie. We'll help you through this."

"I know." Angie smiled. "Like I said, I feel more peace being here with you guys than I've felt at home with my family in months. Years, even."

"Good. Let's focus on that, and the rest will get figured out."

Angie hugged Eve, and they held each other tightly for a few extra seconds.

Finally calm, Angie stood and blew out a steadying breath. "Okay, my dear. I'm going to see what kind of farm-fresh breakfast foods Sonny McPherson has this kitchen stocked with or maybe dive headlong into the Rocky's leftovers. How good was that dinner last night?"

"Unbelievable," Eve agreed. "You go scope it out. I'll be inside in a minute, and we can make breakfast for everyone."

"Sounds good," Angie said. "As soon as I can, I'll be calling Biltmore House to start my search."

"Cool!"

Angie turned and headed into the house, gone barely a second when Eve grabbed her phone and began typing a text to David.

Hi. I know you're doing rounds and you're super busy, so don't worry about responding. I just want you to know how much I love you, and our family, and our life. I miss you so much, and can't wait to see you on Sunday. I'll be thinking of you all day.

She pressed Send and dropped the phone down next to her, fighting her own tears.

Her marriage was wonderful, but so was Angie and Craig's at one time. Eve's familiar fear of failure crept up in her throat and made her nerves fray.

She knew one thing for sure. She needed her

husband to be here. She needed that closeness and quality time and the connection they shared.

Everything would be okay once he was here. They'd relax, reconnect, and remember just how much they truly loved each other.

And maybe she could help Angie do the same for her marriage.

Chapter Nine

Angie

GETTING an appointment with the lead curator at the Biltmore Estate hadn't been that difficult. At first, Angie hit some brick walls, but finally got the voicemail of a woman named Marjorie Summerall, and that's when she decided to drop the name of Angelica Benson, her great-grandmother.

Marjorie had called her back in five minutes, a little breathless with excitement, and invited Angie to come to the Biltmore House during the hour between the daytime and evening Christmas tours of the estate's main house.

Grateful her great-grandmother's name still had some cachet, Angie relaxed during the drive to the Biltmore Estate, shaking off her conversation with Eve, and relishing the fact that her heart felt just the tiniest bit lighter. She was no closer to an answer to her problems or a fix for her broken marriage, but having finally gotten it all off her chest and telling her sister the truth had eased her soul.

Plus, she found it pretty difficult to be anything but joyful as she drove toward the famous estate, soaking up the Asheville vibe that included beautiful views and darling suburban neighborhoods.

She'd borrowed Eve's minivan for her outing, which wasn't exactly like that year Dad bought a convertible for this drive, but she opened a window and let the cold mountain air whip her hair in honor of that memory as she followed the signs to the overpass and down a back road to the Biltmore Estate.

She entered through the main gates, meandered through a treelined road, and gave her name to the guard. He instantly allowed her in, giving directions to a special guest lot behind the House.

She'd done a little research on Biltmore House last night, but all the pictures and a distant memory couldn't quite prepare her for the impact as she rounded a gravel road that wasn't open to tourists, only staff and visitors.

The sprawling estate acreage included a labyrinth of gardens and waterfalls, a winery and stables, a massive hotel and just so many wonderful places to explore. But today, her destination was the crown jewel of the estate, Biltmore House, which, she'd learned from a few Google searches, was a 250-room chateau that was now a treasured museum on par with anything in Europe.

A gasp slipped out as the turrets and cream stone of Biltmore House finally came into view. She had a faint memory of coming here has a child, maybe touring it one summer, but the grandeur had been lost on her at that age.

But not now. The breathtaking limestone castle was topped with spires that reached to the wintry gray sky. A fountain graced the front of the structure and everywhere she looked, there was foliage that she imagined was a thousand shades of green in the summer, and red and gold in the fall.

"Nice place to live and work, Great-Grammy," she whispered as she parked in the back lot, as instructed. A shiver of excitement danced through her at the possibility of finding out even more about the woman.

Aunt Elizabeth knew so little, it had been surprising. She didn't even know about the baby her grandmother had saved, but she did say that her mother, Angie's Granny Jane, didn't look too kindly on the history of the Vanderbilts and their relatives, and had downplayed their role in gifting the land where the cabin had been built.

Angie wasn't sure why—or if it mattered. But she hoped Marjorie Summerall might know more.

As she walked toward the back entrance, Angie welcomed the chilly air and the crunch of gravel under her boots. She tightened her puffer jacket around her and looked up as she walked around the corner to a door marked "Staff Only."

Opening it, she entered a massive vestibule with black and white marble floors, a few pieces of furniture and two long closets.

Almost immediately, an older gentleman in a dress shirt and slacks came out, dabbing his mouth as if she'd interrupted the meal he was sneaking in between tours. "Can I help you?" he asked, clearly not thrilled with the arrival of a stranger in his midst.

"Hi. I'm Angie Messina and I have an appointment with Marjorie Summ—"

"Oh, yes!" His whole face brightened, from the shock of gray hair to his thick white moustache. "She mentioned a guest today. Let me take your coat and I'll take you to her offices."

Whoa, the power of Great-Grandma Benson, Angie thought as she smiled and slipped out of her jacket so he could hang it in one of the closets.

"Have you been to Biltmore House before, Ms. Messina?" he asked as they started down a hallway.

"As a child, I think. But I don't think I've seen this part."

"It's the servants level," he explained. "And not a whole lot different from when your grandmother—no, it must be great-grandmother—worked here."

He knew that? "Yes, great-grandmother. Do you work with Marjorie?"

"I'm a jack-of-all-trades around here—part tour guide, part curator, part Vanderbilt enthusiast." He paused and reached out his hand. "Owen," he added. "Let's get you upstairs to the Winter Garden and you can wait in one of our more beautiful areas."

"All of it is beautiful," she said, the sense of history so strong it felt like arms wrapping around her.

"Indeed it is," he agreed.

They walked up a set of stairs, through another hall, then into a wide open glass-domed sunroom bathed in light and filled with plants. He gestured toward a bench near a central fountain, topped by a stone sculpture.

She slowed her step, soaking up the pure beauty of the place, remembering an art history class she'd taken as an elective in college. She'd ended up loving it more than any other class in her major, and it had led her to a few more history classes before she graduated.

She adored the weightiness of the past, the stories and people and beauty of it all.

"How long have you worked here, Owen?"

"Ten happy years," he told her. "I love this *grande dame*." He swept a hand. "And her history."

"Wow," she said. "That must be a fun job."

"We're very excited about the new project, which I'm sure Ms. Summerall will tell you about. She fairly chirped with anticipation after you called."

Angie lifted a brow, surprised at that. But before she could ask for details, he led her into what the sign said was the banquet hall, which simply took her breath away.

It wasn't just the size and scope, the tapestries or soaring ceiling, but every square inch was decorated in yards of ribbons and thousands of lights. Above a table for at least forty, huge iron circular chandeliers were draped in garlands and poinsettias, with Christmas trees by all of the fireplaces along one wall.

"This is gorgeous," she gushed, pressing her hands together as she tried to take it all in.

"You've barely seen a glimpse of the chateau," he said with a prideful smile. "Please wait here while I go into our administrative office and get Ms. Summerall."

"Of course."

"I'll be right back." He nodded and disappeared

down a hallway, giving Angie a moment alone in the grandeur.

She craned her neck to take it all in, the palatial estate doubly beautiful with the Christmas decorations. Several members of the staff and cleaning crew bustled by, smiling at her as they went about their job in this landmark home.

And it was a home, she remembered. George and Edith Vanderbilt had lived here, raised a daughter here, and entertained family...like the Winchesters. That made her think about Angelica walking these halls, tending to the fire or helping to decorate at Christmas. Really *living* here, not working.

Angie turned at the sound of heels clicking on the marble floor.

A woman strode toward her, gray hair pulled back into a tight bun, wearing a slim gray suit with a crisp white blouse buttoned to the very top. She had one of those timeless faces that could be fifty or seventy-five, but there was warmth in her blue eyes as she extended a friendly hand.

"Ms. Messina, hello. I'm Marjorie."

"You can call me Angie," she said, shaking the woman's butter-soft hand.

"Like your ancestor," she gushed. "How amazing that you were named after her."

"I guess I was. I'm actually Angel, born, if you can you believe it, as a triplet on Christmas Day."

She let her mouth open to a delicate O and pressed her hands together. "I see the extraordinary stories continue through the generations of your family. I'm so pleased to welcome you to Biltmore House."

"I'm thrilled to be here," Angie admitted, glancing around. "And quite impressed."

She laughed easily. "It never gets old, I guarantee you. I've been the head curator for many years and not a day goes by where I don't feel beyond fortunate to work in this exceptional home."

Angie sighed. "I was just thinking that it really was a home, even though it feels like a castle."

"Certainly fit for royalty and legions of servants who made their life easy," she said, nodding to two uniformed staff members who bustled by. "And that's where the fine Mrs. Benson, your great-grandmother, comes in with a very, very special place in the history of this estate."

"I've only just learned that," she said. "My aunt, who would be the only living relative other than my sisters and our families, didn't really know much about Angelica Benson. I found a newspaper article in the attic of our family cabin, and some of her belongings."

Her eyes widened. "We'll want it all."

Angie inched back, not sure what she meant.

Clearly sensing her alarm, Marjorie laughed lightly. "Oh, of course you don't know. Come, let's sit in the drawing room. It's quiet, and the staff is finished checking that room before the evening tours begin. I'll tell you about the project and hope you can help."

Marjorie led them through a corridor, pausing at a billiard room to let her peek in and share some facts about the room in what they called "the bachelor's wing." Chatting about history and art as they passed two Monets—real, honest-to-goodness Monets!—hanging on a wall and three tapestries that could take a week to study, she finally led Angie to a small office.

"This is really the only room on the main floor where we can sit and not deface an artifact," she said. "We work in the basement most of the time, and at the corporate offices in town."

Even this room had the holiday touch, though, with one Christmas tree decorated fully in gold and white standing in the corner. There was a desk, but Marjorie led them to two green velvet sofas.

"So." Marjorie crossed her legs, her gaze locked on Angie. "You said you were looking for information about your great-grandmother. I'm looking for anything that belonged to her. Shall we exchange?"

Still beyond curious, Angie flipped open her purse, deciding to start with the newspaper article. "I found this yesterday, and I'm afraid it's presented more questions than answers."

Marjorie took the paper and eased a pair of reading glasses from her jacket pocket, putting them on to study the article.

"I've seen this," she said. "In an online archive, so I've never touched the newspaper itself." She stroked the paper with reverence, as if it were just as valuable as the words printed on it. "She was certainly a hero."

"That's what I gather. I don't know anything else about her, though, and I'd love to."

Marjorie let out a soft sigh. "What we know is that

she worked here for about five years, as a parlor maid, hired after marrying Mr. Garland Benson."

"My great-grandfather," Angie interjected with pride.

"Garland was a beloved footman for many years. In the winter of 1924, a distant cousin on Edith Vanderbilt's side, Keegan Winchester, along with his wife Louise, their baby daughter Claudia, and some of their staff, were visiting for the Christmas holidays and New Year's celebrations. From the Butler's Log, we've learned that Louise's lady's maid took ill. The house was full with holiday company, so the head butler assigned Angelica as a substitute."

Once again, Angie had to depend on her *Downton Abbey* education, but she suspected this temporary role was likely a big deal.

"Quite an honor," she guessed.

"And quite a responsibility. Should she make a mistake in selecting jewelry or resewing a button, it could have been the end of her time at Biltmore House. And, from what I've gleaned, Louise wasn't an easy woman to please."

"Ahh. So the pressure was on."

Marjorie smiled at that. "Well, Angelica certainly didn't buckle under pressure because she, as the article states, risked her own life to save Baby Claudia during a small fire, so she not only performed well, she was feted for her valor."

Angie smiled with pride, hoping a tiny bit of that courage had been slipped into the family gene pool.

"In fact," Marjorie added, "we understand there was a land gift as a reward."

"It's true," Angie said. "It was six acres along Copper Creek just east of Asheville. They built a cabin that has been in my family ever since. In fact, my sisters and my aunt and I are spending the holidays there."

Marjorie dropped back, her jaw loose. "Well, there's a missing piece of the puzzle. And so wonderful that you still have the home!"

"The original cabin has never left our family. My aunt told me last night that Angelica and Garland raised her mother, my Granny Jane, in that home. Jane married and moved to Raleigh, but never sold the cabin. My mother and aunt spent summers and Christmases there, and that tradition continued when I was a kid. In fact, it's been remodeled and improved as recently as this past year by my aunt."

"Amazing!" Marjorie exclaimed. "I love that."

"It really is," she agreed. "But we had no idea about this history of the original owners. Do you know anything else about her?"

"Quite a bit. But I must say..." She put her hands in the prayer position and pressed them to her chin. "Your timing is quite stunningly perfect."

"Why is that?"

Her eyes danced. "We have funded a restoration of more of the staff quarters, this time on the fourth floor, where the higher-ranking servants lived. This additional space will be added to next year's museum tour. Our research team, along with Vanderbilt descendants, have only just recently decided that one of the rooms to be featured on the tour would be the quarters where Angelica Benson lived with her husband. They were one of the only married couples to ever work and live in the House."

"That is so cool," Angie said on a sigh.

"So you see why your timing is fortuitous. We'd welcome your input on the project, as we love to include family members in this type of thing."

Angie gasped softly, unable to wipe away the smile or calm the chill bumps the invitation gave her. "Seriously?"

"Most definitely," Marjorie assured her. "The one-hundred-year anniversary of that fire and Mrs. Benson's heroic act to save wee Claudia is coming up very early next year. Now that we have an actual descendant of the Bensons, we'd very much like you to record a section of our audio tour that all of our guests listen to on private devices during the self-guided tour."

Angie's jaw dropped. "Really?"

"Absolutely. We love that connection with the past and present. We'll write the copy for you, but we'd love for you to add how that one act of one woman impacted your family, too. That's one of the themes of our museum," she explained. "How events that take place can change the course—for better or worse—of a family's history."

Angie stared at her, a million thoughts swirling in her head, her eyes growing unexpectedly misty.

For a moment, all she could think about was the night when her parents took a spontaneous "date" and met the end of their lives on the way home. Every event, good and bad, carved notches in a family tree, and that's what made life and history and families so fascinating.

"So, it's a very good thing I found that newspaper," she whispered, unable to put her far more philosophical emotions into words just then.

"A very good thing. And I have an accounting of the fire from the Butler's Log, which tells us it really wasn't a major disaster, but it could have been if not for Angelica saving sweet Baby Claudia."

"Baby Claudia," Angie mused. "Was she an important member of the family?"

Marjorie gave a soft laugh. "This is one of the reasons we wanted to commemorate the woman who saved her life. Claudia was a shining example of a life that could impact so many."

"How so?"

"Claudia was a spy in Europe during the Second World War, saving countless lives."

"That's incredible!" Angie gushed.

"Oh, yes. Claudia went on to marry Jonathan Delacorte, who was a speechwriter for President Eisenhower. It has been proven that *she* wrote the speeches, not her husband, and she was the mother of six children and nearly twenty grandchildren, one of whom led the team that invented the Nintendo 64."

"Wait until I tell my nephews," Angie said. "They'll be more impressed with that than the spy and speeches."

Marjorie laughed. "Are they in town with you?"

"They are, for the whole month of December. I

normally live in California, but I'm here and happy to help if it can be done this month."

"If only you could. I so wanted to launch the exhibit on the one-hundredth anniversary of the fire, but that's in just over a month, so such a tight squeeze," she said. "But we will do as much as we can. I'll alert the restoration and historical artifact team today, as well as the tour script writer. You've made my day, Angie."

"Same! And I would absolutely love to help." Angie inhaled sharply, her heart fluttering with excitement at the idea of being a part of this.

"I'll be calling you." Marjorie leaned forward. "And I know this is a bit of a large request, so don't be afraid to say no, but...you mentioned other contents in the box with the newspaper."

"Oh, yes." Angie nodded. "There was a dress, some other clothes, a brooch. Nothing terribly valuable—"

"Every historical item has value," Marjorie interjected. "Would you consider a temporary donation to our museum to honor your great-grandmother's memory in our upcoming exhibit?"

"Absolutely!" Angie felt her whole face light up. "I mean, these were her real items, things she probably had in her room when she lived here. And I'll search the attic for more. I would love to make them a part of the display."

Marjorie clasped her hands together again and beamed at Angie. "I'm so thrilled. The other curators and I are still working on compiling everything we have in our current possession to recreate the Benson Exhibit, as we've called their room. I must admit, it's taken a back-seat to the festivities of Christmas."

"Of course." Angie craned her neck to see yet another chandelier wrapped in ribbons and garland. "The Christmas display is unbelievable."

"Have you taken our tour?"

"In the summer, when I was very young," she said. "I'd probably get a lot more out of it now."

Marjorie just smiled, then stood, and Angie did the same. "Let's check our calendars for when you can bring those items in, okay?"

"Mine's pretty clear," Angie said as they strolled back to the banquet room and Marjorie walked her downstairs to the area where she'd arrived and Owen had hung her coat.

After saying goodbye, Angie stepped into the chilly air and turned, looking back at the chateau, oddly melancholy, considering what an enlightening meeting it had been.

Once again, she had that ache for...*this*.

For Biltmore House? For Asheville? For...*not* California? No, not this time. But for...something. Something... she didn't quite understand.

As she walked to the van, she tried to figure that out and why it mattered right now.

Having met Craig at the age of twenty-one and married him at twenty-three, she never had much of a chance to find her own place in the world. By twenty-four, she was pregnant with Brooke, and that was that.

Angie had loved being a wife and mom...well, until

recently. Until it became shockingly evident that she'd somehow failed miserably at both those roles, and had simply nothing else to put her energy toward.

But today, she felt a passion stir inside her—a longing to be involved in something bigger than herself, to honor that history and impact Marjorie had been talking about. It felt like...a passion. And that was something she'd never really had.

Well, she had it now. At least for the next month. And she had Great-Grandma Angelica to thank for it.

Chapter Ten

Noelle

"I KNOW you're busy with work, believe me, so I really do appreciate you joining me to take these trays to Sonny." Aunt Elizabeth glanced over from the driver's seat of a fairly new SUV, reminding Noelle that she hadn't actually seen her aunt behind the wheel in many years. She was a "car and driver" kind of New Yorker, with preferred-customer status at the limo company.

Looked like those days were gone.

"Why does he need them?" she asked, glancing at the array of metal and porcelain trays in the backseat.

"Church fundraiser," her aunt said, as if that explained it. "Am I taking you away from anything very important?"

"Still waiting for Monmouth to come through on a Yarrow McFarland painting. Oh, and I outbid Collier on a nice deal with a gallery in Chicago this morning," Noelle said brightly, happy to get back on that track they used to share. "East End Gallery. Remember them?"

She lifted a shoulder. "Vaguely. I haven't managed an art deal in forever, Noelle."

"You've just...quit?"

"Well, I was an independent art consultant for nearly two decades. There was no actual 'quitting' involved. I just stopped looking for or accepting new business and deals." She threw Noelle a smile. "I loved it, like you do, but I'm done now. It's a nonstop life, twenty-four-seven with international clients. I'm happy to have it in my rearview mirror."

"You don't miss it?" Noelle asked.

"I have new things in my life," she said calmly.

Noelle stifled a sigh. "I see that."

"You see it, but don't like it," Elizabeth said. "Why don't you come right out and say it, dear?"

"Because..." She threw her hands up, laughing dryly. "Okay. I'm just wondering what happened to the woman who taught me the joys of a solid work ethic, the importance of independence, and the value of a great haircut and good shoes."

She snorted softly. "You don't like my hair?"

"Actually, I love it. But it's...different. I don't like change."

"Also," Elizabeth added, "for the record, I did get a little *frisson* of envy when you showed up in those Loubies."

"Thank you!" she exclaimed.

"But they ruined my feet and did a number on my bank account. And, honestly, I just don't get the same joy from worldly things that I used to."

Worldly? Noelle didn't even know what that meant, really.

"But why did you decide to live here, in the very house you've spent the last two decades avoiding, giving up freedom and a stellar career?"

"I'm free," she shot back. "Free from those shoes and that career and the things that I valued that will simply... end up in an attic covered with dust for Sawyer's grand-children to find. Things that simply don't last. I have found something that spells eternity to me, and I like it."

Noelle dropped her head back, closing her eyes to the view and trying to find the right and most honest words. "It's hard for me," she whispered.

"I realize that. It's one of the reasons I invited you here, to experience the change in person." She gave Noelle a gentle look. "I'm not done teaching you things, my sweet niece."

Noelle turned to face her aunt, trying to soften any harsh words but still share her fears and feelings. "I'm sorry. You know how much I love you and respect you and I don't ever want to hurt you. But, Aunt Elizabeth, is this real or a phase you're going through? And Sonny? I mean, are you sure he's not just after your money?"

She barked a laugh. "Yes, I'm sure. Just as I'm sure that I did have a huge influence on you. I've watched you grow and blossom into a young version of me. Better, even."

"No," Noelle whispered. "No one was better than you."

"Oh, baby girl. You couldn't be more wrong. For one thing, you're in it for the right reasons—you love the art, you love the challenge, and you love your clients. I was in it...as an escape."

"An escape?"

"From losing my sister," she said softly.

Noelle closed her eyes, feeling foolish for forgetting how hard her mother's death must have been for Aunt Elizabeth.

"Sometimes, I don't think about how that accident affected you," she admitted. "I'm sorry. You dropped everything to move to Raleigh and help us through the grief and the rest of high school and you managed to take us somewhere amazing every Birthmas, all while grieving the loss of your sister. You were strong and brave, much more than I would be if anything ever happened to one of my sisters."

Her aunt reached over and put her hand on Noelle's lap. "You were very young and I don't expect you to understand how it impacted my life. During those three years in Raleigh, I numbed my pain by trying to be a substitute for Jackie, and when you all went off to college, I suddenly had...nothing."

"You always had us!"

"But you girls were growing up and starting lives. You didn't need me anymore. That's when it hit me. I went back to art dealing and threw myself into the job and I do mean threw. I dove headlong into the parties and the travel and the fancy stuff. I had that big London client and spent so much time over there, it was just, well, the best escape. But I never, ever faced the pain, at least not until I met Sonny."

Noelle took a deep breath, waiting for her to continue.

"He'd had that same grief, when his wife died twenty years ago. His kids were just about the same age as you three when you lost your parents. Well, a little younger, a little older, but close. But it wasn't nearly as difficult for him because he believes in life after death. He helped me find a new perspective and the kind of peace I'd never known before. I spent my entire adulthood chasing thrills and climbing a career ladder, hoping contentment was at the top of it. But...it wasn't."

The words hit Noelle hard, and she winced. "There's more to life than money," she said softly, reminded of what Angie had said the day before.

"Amen to that!" Elizabeth said. "For me, it's the love of God. And Sonny, but God first."

"Aunt Elizabeth," Noelle said on a soft, gentle laugh. "You were a secular humanist. You always taught me that the only thing I should have faith in is myself."

"I taught you wrong," she replied, so matter-of-fact that it sliced through Noelle, making her feel like her whole world had gone completely upside down.

"I just don't know what to make of any of this," Noelle confessed. "I'm sorry for being hard on you. Obviously, I want you to be happy. It's just that...you've abandoned everything you taught me about happiness."

"Nothing's abandoned," she said. "I'm just a new version of me. A version that doesn't care so much about superficial things, and my priorities have shifted. And,

I'm in love. But I'm still me, Noelle. And I would really, really like it if you got to know Sonny."

After a beat when she realized she had no choice and it was the right thing to do, Noelle sighed. "I will. I promise."

"Start right now, right here, at Red Bridge Farm." She gestured toward the window, bringing Noelle's attention back to her surroundings as Elizabeth pulled into a wide driveway flanked by a huge split-rail fence. "Prepare to fall in love," she added. "I sure did."

Reserving judgment—and love—Noelle took in the rows of pine and spruce trees along the drive, taking them deeper into the property. It was hilly down here, with wide swaths of land for farming and raising animals, lots of fencing, a small silo, and hundreds of trees.

"And here's the bridge that it's named for," Elizabeth announced, driving up to a quaint bridge that crossed a small brook, the red wooden rails standing out against the dusting of snow that had fallen that morning.

Just beyond the bridge, the road split, with one way leading to a large, bright red barn that rose in an A-frame nestled in the pines.

"That's the barn and, beyond it, the stables."

Noelle craned her head to see another building, white with a green metal roof, surrounded by a sturdy fence and a riding ring. But the SUV went in the opposite direction, rumbling up a hill toward a two-story white frame house that sat at the top.

A porch wrapped all the way around the home and the windows were flanked with dark green shutters. A detached garage housed a tractor and the truck he'd been in the other day, but Elizabeth parked in front of the house next to an ancient red truck that had to have been driven off the lot in the 1950s.

Her mind churning from their conversation, Noelle hopped out and took a deep breath, realizing she better take down at least a few of her walls and preconceptions, or else this was going to prove to be a miserable visit... today and the rest of the month.

Besides, she loved her Aunt Elizabeth far too much to let anything get between them. Even...wait. *Whoa.* "Is that a chicken coop?"

"Laying the best eggs you've ever had," Elizabeth said. "Actually, you had them this morning."

"And they were amazing," Noelle agreed.

"There's my Bitsy!" Sonny's Southern drawl floated through the mountain air as he came out to the porch, arms outstretched. Right behind him, Lucky barked and shot out, beating Sonny to Elizabeth.

Instantly, she bent over to greet the dog, letting him lick her hand like it was made of peanut butter, his tail swooshing happily from side to side. Noelle felt her eyes widen, certain she'd seen everything now. Elizabeth Whitaker, famous animal avoider, just got licked.

Laughing, Aunt Elizabeth straightened, coming right into the hug Sonny offered and adding a sweet, loving kiss.

Noelle hung back, giving them their moment, acknowledging she'd never seen her aunt like this with any man. Of course, she'd never been in a serious relationship that Noelle had been aware of, although she'd dated a Greek zillionaire on and off for a few years, and had oodles of male friends.

This was different. This was real and lasting and the ball was in Noelle's court to get to know him and then pass judgment on him.

"Good to see you again, Sonny." Noelle walked over and gave an awkward wave, but he stretched his arms out for a hug.

"Darlin', you're in the South now. We hug hello. Welcome to Red Bridge."

Laughing, she gave him a quick embrace. "It's beautiful," she gushed, and meant it. "And huge."

"It's a sizeable piece of property," he acknowledged. "We got thirty-five acres, horses and livestock, a few sheep, two llamas, some goats, a whole bunch of chickens and plenty of corn, tomatoes, apples, and peaches."

"Wow." She looked around, suddenly realizing that this was no small operation and likely worth a pretty penny. So he either had cash...or needed it to keep this place up. "When did you buy it?"

He chuckled. "I never bought it, I was born to it. This was my daddy's farm, before it got passed down to me. I imagine one day one of my kids will take it over, likely Caroline and her husband, Nate, since he's worked for me forever and knows more about this place than I do. Hannah isn't much interested in the farm, except for the chickens—they're her babies—and my son Christian is more interested in artillery than tractors."

Noelle nodded, remembering his brief mentions of

his kids when they had dinner the night before. But he didn't talk much about himself, so she didn't recall exactly what his grown children did.

"Christian's in the military, right?"

He nodded. "Army. Stationed somewhere in Eastern Europe at the moment, and we're not allowed to ask where or why. Hannah just got here a little bit ago because school let out early today."

"Hannah is the second-grade teacher," Elizabeth reminded her. "And Caroline is here, too? I see her car there."

"She is. The girls—" He grinned and shrugged. "—I call 'em girls even though they're thirty-three and thirty-eight, so forgive me. Anyway, they signed up to make Christmas cookies for a church fundraiser and it seems my kitchen is the best for that. So come on in, ladies. And if you're so inclined, grab an apron and a rolling pin."

He put one arm around Elizabeth and one around Noelle.

"Can you get the trays?" Elizabeth asked him, tipping her head to her SUV. "I scared up seven of them."

"Right on that, then. You go in."

Elizabeth led the way up to the homey front porch, past wicker seating and a swing hanging from the beams and into the warm house. It was just as quaint inside, a genuine farmhouse, not the replicas Noelle had seen on HGTV.

The walls were covered with faded wallpaper and decorated with family photographs in mismatched frames.

The furniture in the living room was soft and a bit worn, but cozy and comforting around a fireplace that crackled with fresh logs. Lucky trotted ahead of them, leading them toward the delicious smell of fresh-baked cookies.

"Bitsy, is that you?" a woman's voice with a soft Southern accent rang out. "I could tell because Lucky has his 'look of love' face."

"I think you've got that dog confused with Dad, Caro," another woman said.

Elizabeth leaned in to whisper, "You're going to love these girls. I want them to be like two more sisters to you."

Noelle just looked at her, not sure how many more people she could meet and promise to love. But if it was what Elizabeth wanted, she'd do her best. "Okay. But don't ask me to bake."

Elizabeth lifted a brow. "Stranger things have happened, baby."

"Yes," she said dryly. "I know."

I<small>T WAS</small> next to impossible not to like Hannah McPherson or Caroline Ellis, and believe it or not, Noelle was actually shaking red sprinkles on sugar cookies within half an hour of arriving.

Hannah, the younger of the two and a second-grade schoolteacher, had soft brown waves that refused to stay in the bright pink scrunchy wrapped around her pony-tail. She was brown-eyed, freckled, effervescent, spunky, and patiently explained exactly how to decorate a cookie to Noelle without being a bit condescending.

Caroline—or Caro, as they called her—was quieter, a mother of one eight-year-old-boy named Joshua, who apparently wanted no part of cookie baking. She had a palpable connection with Elizabeth, which might have made Noelle jealous if Caro wasn't such a genuinely warm person who seemed to care about others more than herself. She had fair coloring, looking a lot like Sonny with her sweet blue eyes, and, whoa, did she know her way around a homemade cookie-making project.

Not long after they arrived and slipped into comfort-able small talk, Sonny got a call from Caro's husband, Nate, that he was needed out in one of the fields. The girls insisted "Bitsy" and Noelle stay for some iced tea and a chat. It didn't take long to realize that Hannah was downright fascinated by Noelle and couldn't ask enough questions about her job, her apartment, her wardrobe, and what she called *The Sex and the City* life.

"Do you go to clubs every night?" she asked. "And shop at fancy boutiques?"

"If I go to a club, it's usually for a client event. I shop in Macy's as often as not."

"Well, Macy's beats the Mast General, where our fashion choices are limited to overpriced Patagonia and T-shirts for tourists," Hannah said. "And the men? Are they all just stupidly rich and living in penthouses?"

"The men might be stupidly rich, but most of the

time the emphasis is on 'stupid.' But if they have seven figures to spend on a painting, I'm happy to take a commission."

Hannah groaned and leaned into her rolling pin. "Dang! I consider it a good day if I didn't get covered in snot by a seven-year-old, and you make million-dollar deals. My stars, my life is dull."

"Mine sounds better than it is many days," Noelle said, surprising herself with the admission. "For instance, my Christmas tradition involves ordering in sushi from my favorite place on Lexington, mixing a nice dry martini, and watching my comfort movie, which is *Spaceballs*."

Hannah snorted at that. "I tried to watch that once and Christian made me turn off the TV and told our mother I was watchin' trash. Maybe I'll stream it tonight."

"Do you live here with your father?" Noelle asked.

She tipped her head and gave a sassy smile. "My life's dull, but not *that* dull, I'm happy to say. I rent a town-house on the outskirts of Asheville near my school, and, yes, before you ask, I have a boyfriend but..."

Suddenly the room was quiet as Caro and Elizabeth exchanged a look.

"But everyone hates him," Hannah said with an exaggerated roll of her big brown eyes.

"We don't hate him," Caro said.

"Well, you don't *like* him."

"He just doesn't appreciate you, Hannah," her sister said. "And I can't help looking out for you. It's my role in this family."

Hannah looked over her rolling pin at Noelle. "They want me married, ASAP. I'll marry when I'm good and ready. And what I like about Keith Kelly is that he is no more interested in marriage than I am."

Instantly, Noelle felt a connection, and she sure didn't expect that. "I feel you, sister. I'm about to be forty and never considered it."

"You might change your mind," Aunt Elizabeth said softly, picking up her phone. "When you meet the right man. Speaking of the right man, Sonny wants to take me out to the north ridge to see the fence he fixed where the sheep keep getting out."

"That sounds fun," Hannah said, perfectly serious before she gave a wide-eyed look to Noelle. "*Not.*"

Noelle laughed at her and looked at Aunt Elizabeth, who seemed unsure if she should go. "You want to stay a few more minutes?" her aunt asked.

Surprisingly, she did. "These cookies aren't going to sprinkle themselves," she joked, making Hannah laugh.

"All righty." Elizabeth stood and, as she passed, she dropped a kiss on Noelle's head. "I knew you had more in common with these ladies than you thought."

After she left, Caro brought a cooled batch of cookies to the butcher block table where Noelle sat, sliding into another chair as she placed the rack next in line for sprinkles.

"Bitsy's told us everything about your folks," she said softly. "I know it was so long ago, but I'm sure it's tough to be back here. I'm so sorry. We know how you feel."

"Oh, thank you." Noelle searched her kind eyes,

thinking of the little she knew about their mother. "Elizabe—" She caught herself. "*Bitsy* said you were about the same age when you lost your mother."

"I was eighteen, and Hannah was just thirteen," she said. "But we knew for some time that she was failing, which doesn't make it better but does make the grieving easier."

Noelle nodded. "The shock of an accident does make it hard to accept, but..." She smiled at the other woman. "Life, sadly, goes on."

"Never the same, though," Caro said.

"So true. Aunt Elizabeth was our saving grace through it all. She's my inspiration, my idol."

"Oh, I can see why. She is one in a million." Caro pressed her hand to her chest. "It's been such fun watching those two sixty-somethings fall in love."

"Is it hard for you?" Hannah asked, coming to the table to join them. "I mean, seeing how much she's changed and fallen so hard in love. I know you two are very close, especially because of your job and all that. Bitsy says you're a carbon copy of her."

Noelle swallowed, closing her eyes, wondering if she was telegraphing her feelings or if these two were just super perceptive. Maybe a little of both.

"It's quite a change, I will say that. I want her to be happy." She looked from one to the other, smiling. "It's nice to know she has you two here."

"How sweet of you," Caroline said, reaching for her. "We can't wait to meet your sisters."

"They're probably better bakers than I am," she said,

lightening the mood and reaching for her phone as it rang.

"Better get that," Hannah said. "Could be a million-dollar deal."

She glanced at the screen, then up at Hannah, whispering the name on the phone. "Stanford Monmouth. Now that man *could* have a million-dollar deal. Can you excuse me?"

"Go, go!" Hannah flicked her hand. "Then come back and tell me what a man named Stanford is like."

"Stupidly rich," Noelle joked as she walked out of the kitchen.

The reception wasn't that much better in this house, so by the time Noelle finally closed the deal to sell an original Yarrow McFarland painting in an all-cash deal, she'd grabbed her down vest and walked far from the house to where she actually got a signal.

She almost pivoted to go back, but the sun was high and the temperature had easily reached the forties, making it simply too beautiful to go inside. Plus, she had so much to think about.

Elizabeth and her new life, and new family. Those lovely ladies and their cookies and warmth. Everyone seemed so happy about this turn of events, so shouldn't she be, too?

As she mulled over all her thoughts, she realized she'd walked to the adorable red barn that seemed to be piled high inside with hay bales. But beyond it, she heard the whinnying of a horse from the stables.

With the exception of the ones that pulled carriages

through Central Park, she couldn't remember the last time she'd seen a horse close up. And she wanted to.

As she got closer and could see inside the stable, she spied the head of a dark brown horse poking out over one of the stall doors. She entered the structure, taking in the high, high ceiling, the long row of semi-enclosed stalls, and a pretty distinct smell of, well, horses and the stuff they make.

But it wasn't bad enough to stop her.

"Hello, there," Noelle whispered to the animal in the closest stall.

He snorted, his giant brown eyes landing on her with so much personality and intent, it nearly took her breath away.

"What's your name, handsome?" she asked, coming right up to the stall, just about face to face with the impressive animal. "I'm Noelle. Maybe you've heard of me?"

He just stared at her.

"I'm the problem child," she said, only half joking. "The one that can't throw my arms around some good old country farm boy who's changed my favorite aunt forever. I don't know, Horsie. Is it me being cynical, or them being too trusting?"

The horse blinked at her, turning a bit as if he had to show off his majestic mane.

She had the weird desire to pet him, but had no idea if that could cost her a finger. But she got as close as she could, feeling comfortable with this particular horse.

"Of course I want her to be happy, more than

anything in the world. But, you know, it hurts me some-how. I don't know why. Maybe because my sisters are married and my parents are gone and all my friends have other things and Elizabeth was that one constant and now she's..."

The horse snorted again.

"Is that you agreeing?" she asked.

"It's him asking for a sugar cube."

She whipped around at the sound of the masculine voice coming from what she'd thought was an empty stall. In a second, Jace Fleming appeared over the wooden doors, holding something out to her.

"Sugar cube," he said. "It's the standard price for counseling around here."

She stared at him, blinked, flushed so hard she was probably the color of the barn, then took the sugar.

"Much cheaper than New York therapists," she said, hating the zing that shot through her when their hands touched.

He laughed softly and pushed the doors open, revealing that he wore filthy gray pants and yet another flannel shirt, his auburn and brown hair mussed from sweat and wind and work. The impact of him made her take a step backwards.

"Sorry to sneak up on you like that," he said. "I was just checking on..." He tipped his head to the stall where he'd been and wiped what looked like mud off of his hands. God, she hoped it was mud. "Athena."

She looked behind him, the stall doors wide open to reveal a white horse lying on the ground. "Is she okay?"

"As okay as you would be if you were eleven months pregnant."

Her jaw dropped. "Eleven..."

"They can go twelve," he said. "But she's getting close. Sonny called this morning and said she was getting restless. Up and down. So I was just checking the foal's position."

Suddenly, the horse rose to her feet, a massive animal, snorting and stomping the ground as she turned to reveal a belly the size of a small country. "Whoa. That's...pregnant."

He laughed softly and glanced at the horse. "She means that with kindness, Athena." He turned back to her and stage-whispered, "She's very cranky and does not like to be called fat."

She couldn't help laughing as she looked at the man who somehow wore dirt and sweat like a badge of honor. "I did not call her fat," she said, very serious. "Just pregnant."

"Why don't you give Jasper his payment and I'll let you come and tell Athena you're sorry."

She turned and lifted the sugar cube, opening her palm, giggling a little when the horse sucked it right out of her hand. "Oh! Okay. Thanks for the advice, Dr. Jasper. I'm going to go visit your colleague now."

Smiling, she followed Jace into the next stall, where Athena had once again lowered her hefty body to the ground.

"See?" he said. "This is a restless mare ready to get the show on the road."

The floor of the stable was covered in dirt and hay and mud, but something told her it was worth a smudge on her formerly perfect white sneakers. She followed him in, getting closer to the horse, who stared ahead as if looking up would just be too much for her right then.

"Wow, hello, gorgeous." Noelle crouched down, close to the horse. She was so captivated by Athena's size she hardly noticed the smells of musk and manure, and forgot about the dirt.

"She's something, isn't she?" Jace joined Noelle in a crouched position, patting Athena on the back of her neck.

"She's definitely got a pregnancy glow, that's for sure." She looked at Jace. "Can I touch her?"

"Absolutely. She would never admit it, but she needs attention right now."

Noelle lifted her fingers to gently stroke against the horse's soft, white coat, which was speckled with delicate gray spots.

Jace glanced at her, his slightly crooked smile transporting her back...to a fifteen-year-old girl sitting by that creek with him petting Rascal, feeling all the things for a boy.

"She likes you."

She liked...*him*. Then and, honestly, a little bit now.

He reached up to pet Athena, too, his fingers brushing Noelle's just enough to give her a shiver.

"Have you ever ridden a horse?" he asked.

"Not for many, many years," Noelle said. "I can't remember how old I was when my parents took us horseback riding. And now? Well, it's not exactly a common activity in the Upper East Side."

"Would you like to?" Jace glanced behind him at the other horse in the stable. "Riding is one of Jasper's favorite treatments for people who have trust issues." At her look, he angled his head in a silent apology. "I didn't eavesdrop on purpose."

"I know. And I don't have trust..." Well, yes, she did. Trust issues galore. She lifted a shoulder. "Okay, a few. And as far as riding?" She studied his face, lost in the darker rims of gray around his blue irises and all the memories those eyes held, magnetically drawn to him the way she had been as a young teenager. "I suppose I could give it a go."

"Good." Jace patted Athena's strong neck but kept his gaze on Noelle. "Why don't you, um, give me your number and we'll set something up?"

Her heart gave a little jump at the request, but she managed to have a steady hand as she typed her number into the phone he handed her.

As they both stood, Jasper snorted, getting her attention.

"Your therapist approves of this decision," Jace teased. "And so do I."

She smiled at him, and still had that grin on her face all the way back to the farmhouse, where she sprinkled more cookies, laughed with Hannah and Caro, and felt her whole heart thaw like yesterday's snow in today's sunshine.

Chapter Eleven

Eve

"Sure I can't interest you in coming to church with us?" Sonny looked over his shoulder at Eve as he stoked the fire in the living area. "I know we got some snow last night, but my truck can handle anything."

"Thank you, but David's on his way." Her smile wavered as she considered his words. "Are the roads bad? I wouldn't want him to have any problems."

"What's he driving?"

"An Audi sedan, but it has four-wheel drive."

"He'll be fine." Sonny stood, brushing off his dark dress pants. "Will he be here for a few days? We'll be cutting down the tree later this week when it warms up a bit, and we'll need another man to help carry the load."

"What?" Sawyer's voice, far too loud for nine in the morning, echoed through the great room as he practically flew down the stairs and sock-skated to them. "We're cutting down a tree?"

Sonny looked at him, chuckling and shaking his head. "Kid, you got more energy than a newborn puppy."

He grinned and made a muscle with his tiny biceps. "Strong like a bear, too!"

Eve laughed and Sonny pointed at him. "You're gonna love my grandson, Joshie," Sonny said. "He's a pistol just like you."

"You have a pistol, Uncle Sonny?" Sawyer asked, wide-eyed. "Can I shoot it?"

"Yes and no," he replied.

"Do we use an axe to chop down the tree? Can I swing it?"

"Same answer, yes and no." Sonny reached out and gave Sawyer a high-five. "Say good morning to your mama, son."

"Morning, Mommy." He turned from bear hunter to little boy, crawling up to cuddle with her on the sofa.

"Hi, honey." She pressed a kiss on his curly mop. "How'd you sleep?"

He made a face and lifted a shoulder. "I think I heard a bear, so I had to watch out my window for a while. He was too scared to show up."

Sonny laughed, then his face grew serious. "We could see one in the woods when we cut down the tree."

"We could?" And he was off the sofa again, on his tiptoes. "That'd be cool!"

"What would be cool?" Aunt Elizabeth came in from the hall that led to her bedroom, wearing a lovely navy dress, a wool coat draped over her arm. It was the first time Eve had seen her in anything but overalls or jeans since they'd arrived, and she reminded Eve of days gone by, when Elizabeth and Jackie would dress up for dinner or a special occasion.

The pang of missing her mom surprised Eve, since she'd certainly had plenty of encounters with more poignant memories these past few days while they'd decked the halls.

"We're cutting down a tree!" Sawyer announced. "In the forest! With an axe!"

"Of course we are! It's an Asheville Christmas cabin tradition," Elizabeth said with a laugh, making Eve wonder why her aunt didn't get those pangs—or if she did, how she seemed to sail through them. "Where are the others?" Elizabeth asked.

"Noelle is sleeping, so are the older boys, and Angie is...in the attic, I think."

"More Christmas decorations?"

"Angelica Benson research," Eve explained. "Apparently the lady from the Biltmore Estate wants to see her today."

"On a Sunday?" Sonny asked.

"She said it's the quietest day during the week while the Christmas tours are going on. Angie's taking what she's found in the attic for the exhibit."

"Well, more power to her," Elizabeth said. "As I told you, I don't think I've been in that attic five times in my life. My mother? Yes, she stuffed everything up there. And your mother was fearless and the keeper of all things Christmas. I'm sorry I can't help Angie more."

"It's fine," Eve assured her. "The whole thing has consumed her and, honestly, it's been good for her."

What Eve didn't want to say in front of Sawyer was that the project had been a welcome diversion for Angie, taking her mind off her troubles at home.

"I'll go up and help after church if you like," Sonny offered.

"No, no," Elizabeth said. "But you can hang the outside lights later this week."

"I'm planning on it, ma'am," he said with a wink. "But first, let's not be late for church."

They said another goodbye and headed out while Eve made some breakfast for Sawyer and more coffee for herself. After Sawyer disappeared to wake his brothers, she checked the phone repeatedly for word from David.

There'd been a good two-inch snowfall overnight, but before she had a chance to stress too much, she heard a car outside.

With a soft hoot of relief, she headed straight to the front door, no jacket or shoes, her whole body aching to see him.

He must have been just as anxious, throwing open the driver's-side door and launching from the car to meet her on the porch with a hug that took her completely off the ground.

"Oh, I missed you so much," she cooed, her face buried into the layers of his jacket.

"Evie, babe, I missed you, too." David kissed the top of her head. "And this mountain? The scenery? The road on the way in? It's all so much more beautiful than I imagined."

Eve finally willed herself to pull away from his

embrace, just far enough to glance around the snow-covered property, seeing it through her husband's eyes for the first time.

"I can't believe we've never been out here, even just to see it from the road. I know I never wanted to, but I'm so glad Aunt Elizabeth made this happen."

"You doing okay?" he asked, searching her face. "All the memories and stuff?"

"Oh, I'm fine!" She flicked her wrist as if to say nothing could bother her. "Watching the boys gobble up every single experience has been amazing. Being with my sisters is priceless and I forgot how much I love it here."

"So happy to hear that." He put a tender hand on her cheek. "I've been worried about you."

She leaned her head into his chest, grateful for the concern, but confident that deep inside, she'd done a spectacular job of burying her decades-old pain.

"So, check it out." She pulled him into the house with a sweeping gesture. "The log cabin with a fire. The decorations are not quite complete—obviously, there's a tree missing. But it's been slow, since Noelle is always working, Angie's on a mission, and the boys just want to play outside."

"I'll help while I'm here," he promised. "And where are those boys of mine?"

"Daddy!" Sawyer's shriek came right on cue, with Bradley and James right behind him, all of them still in their pajamas, the three of them rushing down the stairs to greet their father.

"Hey, kiddos!" He instantly crouched down,

throwing Sawyer onto his shoulder as he hugged Bradley and gave James a big high-five.

Angie and Noelle weren't far behind, coming in to say hello. They all chatted and filled him in on what he'd missed, from the hiking to the decorating to the pregnant horse and the alleged bear that Sawyer swore was stalking the property, even though James and Bradley insisted he was making it up.

"And there's a dog!" Sawyer announced, draping himself over David's back like it might get him a ride. "Named Lucky. He belongs to Uncle Sonny!"

"Uncle?" He lifted a brow. "That didn't take long."

"Things happen fast out here," Eve said on a laugh.

After they ate and relaxed, Noelle and Angie insisted on cleaning up so the five members of the Gallagher family could take a long walk and show David the property. As they walked in the freshly fallen snow, Eve slipped her hand into David's and leaned her head on his shoulder, deeply content to have him here.

"How many days can you stay?" she asked as they strolled along the icy creek and the boys shot in and out of their view in front of them, already starting to throw snowballs.

"I think I'm good until Wednesday night," he said. "I'll have to go back for two days, then I can be back on Saturday."

"Awesome. You'll be here for the tree lighting in town," she said, smiling up at him. "It's new, but I understand it's a big Asheville thing that the boys will love."

"That sounds great," he said. "I'm on call that weekend, but I'm going to hit up John Bellasario to back me up so I won't be tied to my phone." He leaned down and kissed her. "I've missed you so much."

"Oh, honey, I've been so worried," she admitted.

"About what?"

"About our distance."

"I'm three hours away, Evie. And a simple text."

"I know, I know. But I hate to bother you. Anyway, Angie and Craig are having problems and—"

"What kind of problems?" he asked.

"Big ones. They barely speak, he's shut her out of his life, and Brooke is going through a teenage phase that would curl your hair if she were your daughter."

He cringed. "Eesh. That's hard. How's Angie handling it?"

"Diving into the past."

He gave her a quizzical look and she told him more details about the discovery of Angelica Benson's heroism at Biltmore House, plus Angie's involvement with the project to create an exhibit about the woman.

"And no one knew this?" he asked, surprised. "Not your aunt or your mother?"

"If my mother knew it, she never mentioned it. Aunt Elizabeth says her mother, Granny Jane, who was Angelica's daughter, was always a bit dismissive of the whole thing. Maybe she was embarrassed that her mother worked for the rich people and they lived out here in a log cabin. I don't know."

"Yeah, 'cause this would be just horrible to have to live here," he joked.

"Well, compared to Biltmore House, it's rather pedestrian. But the whole thing has been great for Angie, since when she's not mired in the past, she's worried about the future."

"Poor thing. How's Noelle doing? You said she was struggling with the new and improved...what did you say the farmer called your aunt? Bitsy?" He choked. "I can't imagine her accepting that."

"More than accepting. She's embraced the whole Bitsy vibe," she said on a laugh. "But Noelle's better. She's trying to come to terms with the change, which she admits she hates, and she's spent a little time with a cute boy—"

"Excuse me?"

"I mean, he *was* a cute boy when were fifteen and she used to hang out and kiss him, but now he's forty, widowed, and a veterinarian with a little girl."

He lifted his brows with a curious look. "So Angie's discovered her new passion, Noelle's flirting with the locals. What has my beautiful wife been doing this past week?"

"Missing you. Herding boys. And..." She looked around, the chill in the air reaching into her bones. She'd also been worried about their marriage, which sounded so silly right now, she didn't even want to say it out loud.

"Evie..." he prodded, knowing her so well.

"You know, I'm..."

He slowed his step and looked down at her, putting a finger under her chin. "Truth or I tickle."

She laughed at the old joke they'd shared since before

they were married. "Good luck getting through this down jacket."

"So you *are* hiding something."

"No, no. Not hiding. I'm just..." She blew out a breath. "Marriage takes work."

He drew back, obviously not expecting that. "And..."

"I'm worried that you work more on, well, *work* than on us."

He held her gaze with his mesmerizing hazel eyes, his expression softening. "I don't want you to worry. I'm here, and we are not Craig and Angie."

"I didn't say that."

"You didn't have to." He lowered his face to give her a kiss, parting his lips to deepen the contact and—

Wham! A fat, wet snowball smacked Eve's back.

"Stop smooching!" James hollered. "And start throwing!"

Instantly, they stepped back from each other, sharing a look and a smile. Without saying a word, they both bent over, scooped snow, and started packing.

"Snow fight!" Sawyer yelled, throwing himself on the ground to make snowballs. "Bigs versus littles!"

"Guess we're the bigs," David deadpanned, lining up his first shot. He whipped it at Bradley's knees, a direct hit.

"Dad!" Bradley giggled, buckling a bit.

In a flash, Eve got her snow in a pack and looked from James to Sawyer, wondering which one would make the easiest target. She went for James, sailing a snowball that brushed his arm.

"Weaksauce, *Mamacita!*" he called, running toward her with a toss that landed right on her shoulder, exploded and soaked her face with snow.

Laughing, she retaliated while David got off a few great hits, always at Bradley's legs.

"You're down, man," he called, cracking up as Bradley dramatically fell in the snow.

Eve took another hit, falling to her knees and looking around, doing a mental headcount, as mothers do. "Hey, where's Sawyer?"

They all stopped and turned, looking.

"He went to find 'better snow,'" Bradley announced with an eye roll. "As if it's better over there."

"I'll go find him," James said, looking at what appeared to be his brother's footsteps in the snow.

"I'll come!" Bradley followed.

"And in the meantime," David said with a tease, "I'll take down my partner." With a big grin, he came at her flinging snow, making her laugh so much she tumbled into the ground, right on her back, her neck suddenly cold and wet from contact with the snow.

"And she's down!" he exclaimed, falling on his knees in front of her and onto his hands, bracing them on either side of her head so he was right on top of her.

Neither said a word, the only sound their trapped breaths of exertion and anticipation.

"I might," he said, "have to kiss my prisoner."

She laughed again, biting her lip. "I might have to let you."

With a soft moan, he closed the space between their faces to let their lips brush.

"A bear! A bear!" Sawyer's voice echoed through the trees. "I saw him!"

Immediately, David sat up and looked around, both of them spotting James and Bradley flanking their little brother.

"There is no bear," James called. "Just his ridiculous imagination."

They each took an arm and lifted Sawyer, making him run in the air with his legs like little eggbeaters.

"I saw him! Big, black, very dangerous."

Eve propped up on her elbows, watching the three of them come closer, suddenly awash with a memory so intense it took her breath away.

Running with Angie and Noelle, right there, in the same spot, with the same amount of snow, with the same sibling love that her boys shared.

And Mom and Dad were right about...here. Not laying in the snow about to kiss, but doing something together, staring at their daughters, loving them with the same intensity that Eve felt this very minute.

Little did they know that in a few short years, they'd be gone and—

"Man, I love those kids," David murmured, staring at their sons. When she didn't answer, he turned to her. "Evie?" he asked, his face shifting from joy to concern. "Honey, why are you crying?"

She didn't know how to answer that. Because life was short and sometimes unfair? Because she would give anything for her parents to have met her husband and sons? Because sometimes it really, really hurt to be here.

"Eve?" He touched her cheek. "What?"

"I'm just happy," she said, blinking back tears and hoping he didn't see through that explanation. "So happy you're here."

"Me, too," he said, leaning close to plant a light kiss on her lips. "I love you."

"I love you, too."

And just at that moment, the hurt took baby steps closer to healing.

Chapter Twelve

Angie

The fourth floor of Biltmore House was hushed when Owen walked her up there, carrying the plastic bin of treasures she'd brought for today's meeting. He'd explained that ten of the rooms were on the normal tour, but not included in Christmas. And here, they would be opening several more, including the Benson Exhibit.

The corridor of work and sleep rooms for the staff was dimly lit and cool, a mix of areas that looked exactly like they might have a hundred years ago and rooms that were clearly being used to manage museum artifacts.

He took her into what he called a folding room, part of the staff laundry wing, where there were wide counters along each wall and a huge table in the middle. On nearly every surface were artifacts and items, some laid out, some still in containers.

While Angie waited for Marjorie, she perused the treasures, but in her mind she imagined her great-grandmother in this room, maybe using the very iron that Angie had found in the attic. She'd also discovered a tea set and a locket engraved with the letter A and a picture of a baby inside. All of those items were tucked into the bin she'd brought, along with the metal storage box that she'd found under the floorboards.

"Angie, it's so nice to see you again." Marjorie breezed in, wearing a navy version of her business suit, just as professional on a Sunday as she'd been the last time Angie was here. She reached both hands out to take one of Angie's in a warm greeting. "Oh, you're cold. Winter has really come to Asheville, hasn't it?"

"After California, I think it's kind of exhilarating," Angie told her, glancing around. "Or maybe that's just because I'm back here. I do love this place."

"It speaks to some people more than others and with your familial connection, I'm not surprised the House—that's what the locals call it—is speaking loud and clear to you." She gestured toward the plastic bin. "And you come bearing some gifts. I'm so excited to see it all!"

"I wish I could have found more, but sometime in the last century, that attic must have been cleaned. I couldn't find much older than, say, the 1950s. But there are a few things, and the original box I found."

"Shall we?" Marjorie practically rubbed her hands together in anticipation.

Angie lifted the yellowed paper from the top. "So, you saw the newspaper the other day when I stopped by. I brought it back."

"We'll frame it." Marjorie tenderly took the paper, admiring the photo that accompanied the article about Angelica's heroic act of bravery. "Oh, my assistant reached some descendants the other day to talk about this exhibit."

"Really? The guy who helped invent the Nintendo 64?" She laughed. "As I suspected, my nephews were pretty excited."

"His brother, a man named Garrett Delacorte, one of Claudia's many grandchildren. He was the only one who returned Diana's call, and was extremely interested in finding out more about Angelica and her offspring. I imagine he'll come for the grand opening of the exhibit, if not before. We'd like to get him to record some audio, too, if possible."

"I'd love to meet him," Angie said, reaching in to pull out the brooch she'd wrapped in tissue. Revealing the peach porcelain shaped like a flower with tiny pearls and diamonds inside, she added, "My sister and aunt are both art dealers and this is an enameling technique called...bass..."

"*Baisse-taille*," Marjorie finished. "It's a certain way of carving that gives you this glorious translucence." She held it up to show Angie how it allowed light through the petals. "And I know exactly where she got it."

Angie blinked at her. "You do?"

"I'll tell you in a moment," she said, setting the brooch carefully on the counter. "Is that clothing?"

"I think it's a dress, but I didn't unwrap it yet," Angie said. "I didn't want to ruin delicate fabric and I figured you have experts here."

"That was smart. We need to handle everything carefully, but we can take a peek." She gently removed the white tissue and together they unfolded a long green velvet gown, draping it over a settee so they could admire it.

"This belonged to a parlor maid?" Angie reached to graze her finger over the gorgeous fabric and gold button accents down the bodice.

"My guess is that it belonged to Louise Winchester, and was something else she gave Angelica to thank her for saving Baby Claudia. Look at the workmanship on the lace cuffs. That's a lady's dress, not one for a lady's maid."

"Not bad for a hand-me-down."

Marjorie laughed. "Louise probably wore it once, but for Angelica? This would have been her formal dress. She probably donned it for the Biltmore staff holiday events, given the material and the color."

"A Christmas dress." Angie sighed, picturing her great-grandmother all dolled up in velvet and lace. "I love it."

"We'll hang it in a place of honor in her room exhibit."

As she sifted through the rest of the treasures, Marjorie cooed lovingly over every one, able to provide a story about almost all of them, or explain how they came to be part of Angelica's life and then offered to show more to Angie in another room.

"This isn't all of it?" Angie asked.

"Good heavens, it's barely the tip of the iceberg. We're doing multiple new exhibits, not just the Benson room. It's all down the hall, now. Come with me. There are several items that belonged to your great-grandfather there, so I think you'll love it."

A short walk brought her into a large room that instantly felt like an extremely disorganized antiques store. A massive table that had to seat ten or twelve was draped in black velvet and covered with clothes, art, and jewelry, and all along the walls were dressers, small tables, and one oversized armoire.

Under one section was a handwritten sign that read, "Garland and Angelica Benson."

"We have quite a bit on Garland, since he worked here for ten years before marrying Angelica and bringing her into the house," Marjorie explained as she gestured toward a black suit. "But you're really helping us beef up Angelica's portion of the exhibit."

"When did they move out of this house and into the cabin?" Angie asked. "We know that the original cabin was built around 1928 or 1929. Did they live there or here?"

"We don't know," Angie said. "Many of the servants lived in their own homes around town, and came here to work a shift but not live here. But Garland was not merely a footman, but a substitute valet. There's no record of them in the house in the 1930s but as we moved into the Great Depression, many of the jobs changed or were cut back. There's no record of when they left these quarters, but we know that Angelica could not have worked pregnant. When was your grandmother, her daughter, born?"

"My aunt says around 1930, but we don't know the exact day or year."

"That's probably when they moved out, then. Before that, this was her dressing table."

She led Angie to a very small oak vanity with a nicked and scarred top.

"Her very table?" Angie ran her fingers over the carved edges and touched the small white enamel drawer pull. "May I?"

"Of course."

She slid the drawer out, sighing when she saw it was empty. "I don't know what I expected to find."

"You expected to find this." She turned and lifted a picture frame, handing it to Angie. "It's a letter from Louise to Angelica."

Taking it, Angie squinted to make out the ink on the parchment.

My dearest Mrs. Benson,

Although it has been nearly six months since we left the Biltmore Estate, I want you to know that I think about you and your bravery on a daily basis. Because you were willing to risk your own life, my baby is alive today. She's crawling, laughing, sleeping so beautifully, and I expect she'll take her first steps in a month or so. Have I thanked you enough?

I know my husband gifted you with land, but that came with such stipulations and using it requires you to build a home. Is that really a gift or a monumental project? This morning, I came across this brooch that belonged to my Great-Aunt Matilda. It's always been a favorite of mine, but I want you to wear it with the knowledge that it is steeped in my appreciation and respect.

Someday I will tell dear Claudia that her life is a blessing, granted by a parlor maid at the Biltmore House. Her children, and her children's children, will owe you a debt of gratitude for generations to come.

With my deepest affection,

Mrs. Keegan J. Winchester

For a long moment, Angie stared at the signature, chills rising on her arms. "So that's where she got the brooch."

"It appears so," Marjorie said softly. "The ancillary exhibits are changed every one to two years. Then it will be back in your family."

She smiled and set the frame down. "I know it's in good hands here."

"It is, although..." Marjorie gave a laugh and turned. "You wouldn't know that by looking at the chaos that is this room."

"I'm sure it's not chaos to you."

Marjorie slid her a dubious look. "If only that were true. Sadly, my staff, which is small, is completely focused on the Christmas tours. My people are pulled left and right and I can't seem to make headway on this process. It's looking more and more doubtful we'll make a January tenth grand opening."

"The anniversary of the fire," Angie said, nodding. "Is that so important?"

"From a PR standpoint it is," Marjorie said. "We could generate more news stories with that hook, especially if we have those audio recordings from you and Garrett Delacorte, Baby Claudia's grandson." She gave a soft laugh. "*Baby* Claudia who lived to be eighty-seven. She'll always be Baby Claudia to me."

Angie smiled at that, looking around with a different perspective based on what Marjorie had said. "So, this isn't controlled chaos? It's just...chaos?"

"I'm afraid so, but please, don't worry about your belongings. They're perfectly safe here. No one will touch them. That, I suppose, is the problem. I need someone to touch them, to catalogue every single item, take pictures, do research on age and origin, and put everything into some semblance of order."

"Oh, that sounds..." Like so much fun, Angie actually got a little shiver of envy for the person who had that job.

"Right—daunting." Marjorie shook her head.

"Actually, I was going to say it sounded like a blast." Angie laughed. "I mean, it beats the dusty old attic I've spent the last few days exploring."

Marjorie started to say something, then stopped, eyeing Angie as if she had a thought. "You know..." Then she shook her head. "Never mind."

"What?" Angie asked, intrigued by the sparkle in the other woman's eyes.

"It was just a crazy idea," she said. "You're here on a holiday with your family, so...forget about it."

Angie's heart did a little jump. "I have time," she said. "I can do the audio recording for you. I can do anything for you."

"I'm beginning to get that impression. Would you be willing to...volunteer?"

"To do the cataloging and pictures and research?" Angie's brows lifted.

"Right? It's too much," Marjorie said, misreading the question in Angie's voice. "Insane to even think it, but I couldn't pay, so—"

"Yes!" The word shot out so fast, Marjorie actually drew back in surprise. "I would volunteer. I would love to volunteer!"

Marjorie laughed softly, probably because Angie sounded a little desperate.

"This whole thing fascinates me," Angie confessed. "Not just because this exhibit is dedicated to my great-grandparents, but this house, this history, this...everything. I feel like I belong here. I love it so much, and if you want me to spend a few hours taking pictures and making order out of this chaos? Honestly, I'd love to."

Marjorie fought a smile, her gaze pinned on Angie. "You remind me of myself long ago," she said softly. "I recognize the passion for the past, and it's a beautiful thing."

"I'll take that as a compliment. And...a yes? I can do it. I can get bonded or be fingerprinted or whatever you need to do for new volunteers, but...please don't make me beg."

Laughing, Marjorie surprised her by reaching out and pulling Angie in for a quick hug that seemed both genuine and wildly out of character.

"I'm a sucker for enthusiasm," she confessed. "No begging necessary. Let's get the process started."

"Oh, my gosh, thank you!"

"No, thank you! Oh, and wait. One more thing. Can you stay here one moment?"

"Of course. I'll plan my first day on the job."

As Marjorie hurried out of the room, Angie stood stone still, as if moving one inch could make her wake up and realize it was all a dream. A volunteer job to help create the exhibit honoring her great-grandparents! It was, well, dreamy.

"All righty," Marjorie said as she strolled back in, pulling Angie out of her thoughts. In her hand was a small envelope. "It's not actual pay, which I can't offer, but please take these. A dozen tickets to the Christmas tour, with a private guide and access to many parts of the House that others don't get to see. Those are impossible to come by, so please enjoy with all the family you have here."

Angie gasped softly. "I'm touched, Marjorie. Thank you."

"Thank *you*, Angie. I'll email you some paperwork, and you will have to get bonded, which we can do here, and we'll have you ready to roll next week."

This time, it was Angie who hugged the other woman spontaneously. "I'm so excited."

She was still smiling as she left, stepping out into the chilly air with a light heart and high hopes for this little adventure into the past, which she believed would somehow brighten the future.

Chapter Thirteen

Noelle

NOELLE CLOSED her fingers around the chilly steering wheel of Eve's van, gripping it with the same tension that had a hold on her heart. She wasn't sure why an afternoon of horseback riding with Jace made her a little nervous, but it did.

She glanced at her phone screen, following the GPS route back to Red Bridge Farm, taking a deep, calming breath. Maybe she wasn't *nervous*. No, this was more like a hum of anticipation—like she was when she had to negotiate a deal or win an auction for a client.

She wasn't dreading this day, by any means. In fact, maybe she was looking forward to it a little too much. Could that be what had her on edge? The feeling that her pesky glimmer of a crush on Jace was starting to become undeniable, no matter how many times she swore to herself it was no more than teenage memories.

And since their "relationship" absolutely couldn't go anywhere, the feelings seemed kind of silly and wrong and...yeah. Impossible to ignore.

She passed the darling bridge and turned toward the

barn, rumbling over a gravel road to find Jace outside the stables, strapping a saddle onto a tan horse she hadn't seen before. Not that she had her attention on the horse, who might have been beautiful, but not as easy on the eyes as the man next to it.

No flannel today. He wore jeans, and a soft blue shirt under a down vest, the sun highlighting the red and gold streaks in the brown hair that fluttered over the collar.

He was...well, not like any of the men she knew in New York. So masculine and comfortable in his skin, with broad shoulders that seemed made for a woman to rest her head on.

She could still see the ghost of a fifteen-year-old boy in him, the way he shook back a lock of hair or moved with an innate grace he'd had even then. But more than that, she could see a great-looking, good-hearted man who...made her question every decision she'd ever made.

Should she have called him after her parents died? Would their budding teenage romance have blossomed into something deeper? Could Jace have been the man to make her turn her back on Aunt Elizabeth's precious "independence" and choose a life more like Eve and Angie's, with a husband and kids?

Or had Noelle Chambers been destined for the life she now led, no matter what had happened in her past?

She wasn't sure, but something told her today, she might find out. Or she'd just have a great time riding horses in the sunshine with an old friend. Yeah, that would be good, too.

"You made it!" Jace patted the horse's neck before

jogging over to where Noelle had parked outside of the ring.

As she climbed out of the front seat, she caught his gaze dropping over her, lingering a split second before meeting her eyes. The smile widened and she could have sworn she saw some judgment in his eyes.

"What? Too nice for riding?" She glanced down at her faded straight-leg jeans—yes, they were expensive and came from Barney's, but they were just jeans. She'd picked a cable-knit sweater with a tan leather jacket and her boots—not red-bottoms, thank you very much—had the lowest stacked heels she could find without borrowing Aunt Elizabeth's. "It's as casual as I get unless I was expected to show up in pajamas and slippers."

"I'm not complaining," he said, coming closer. "You look...great." The word seemed to catch in his throat and made her heart hitch.

"Oh, okay. Thanks."

He reached his arms out for a hug, which she accepted, willing herself not to notice the fact he smelled like woods and sunshine and mountain air.

"So, am I going to regret this?" she asked.

Inching back, he frowned. "I hope not. Are you scared of horses?"

She was scared of...feelings. And being this close to him brought out a whole host of them. "Not really, but I'm no expert. Should I wear a helmet?"

He laughed. "Cassie has to, but I don't think you're at any risk of being flung from the saddle. You might have fun, though."

"Fun, huh?"

"What do you normally do for fun?" he asked.

She laughed. "I work a lot. Like, more than your average person, I guess."

He looked a little surprised. "And you like that?"

"Usually. But I'm up for a new kind of fun..." She glanced at the horses. "Which, I have to be honest, doesn't usually involve large animals or the outdoors."

Jace led her to the large pen where two big, beautiful horses were meandering about, both wearing saddles and bridles and looking ready to gallop away.

"Well, large animals and the outdoors are basically my specialties, so I'll be your fun guide today," he said.

Noelle locked eyes with him for a second, not having a quip to fling back because...were his eyes always that beautiful? Maybe it was the creases at the edges that weren't there at fifteen. They spoke of a life of sunshine and laughter and made her a little jealous that she didn't get enough of either of those.

"And I," she finally said, "am your willing participant today."

He put a hand on her shoulder and guided her toward one of the horses. "Now, you met Jasper, as I recall, a couple days ago."

She recognized the horse's coloring and the spirit in his big brown eyes as he looked at her.

"That's Dr. Jasper, my personal four-legged shrink." She took a few steps closer, feeling more vulnerable around the beast without the stable door to protect her.

"How are you doing, Jasper? Come up with a diagnosis for me yet?"

"He thinks you're a workaholic," Jace said, giving her a half-smile as he brushed his hand over Jasper's mane. "Treatment plan includes getting in the saddle, enjoying the weather, letting the wind blow through your hair, and forgetting you even have a job."

"Hey, I'm here." She held her hands up. "Computer-less."

"It's a sight for sore eyes, that's for sure."

"Where's Cassie?" Noelle asked, glancing around. "No goats on a leash?"

He chuckled. "She's with her grandparents. My folks are still in the area, and they take her every chance they get."

"Oh, your mother and father are so sweet. How are they?"

"Pushing seventy and as feisty as ever. They were pretty excited you were back in town."

"Me?" She blinked at him, not sure what surprised her more—that his parents remembered her or that he was talking about her to them. "How nice that they even know my name."

He snorted. "Please. They were there for the great unraveling of Jace Fleming."

Looking up at him, her jaw loosened. "You...unraveled?"

He answered with a shrug, then turned to the other horse, the lighter, caramel-colored beauty. "This is Rosie. She was in the pasture when you were in the stables, but she is an absolute doll. Good-hearted, ready to please, and extremely sensitive with new riders. Cassie learned on her, so you're in good, uh, saddle with this one."

"Hello there, Rosie. You're a pretty thing. So, I'm not riding Jasper?"

"Nah. He's an occasional wildcard and not the best for a first-timer. But no matter what, you can just relax. I'll be with you the entire time, Noelle."

She took a deep breath as he said her name, surprised that it still had an impact on her, the way it had long ago. The way it sounded when he whispered it when they first held hands and realized that their childhood friendship, however limited to Decembers and summertime, had grown into something more.

"Okay." She swallowed. "I'm ready."

"Good. I'll help you on. Give me your hands."

Noelle lifted her hands, suddenly a bit nervous to be putting so much trust in such a powerful animal. But the second she placed her fingers into Jace's palms, her tension eased.

"Now, left foot in the stirrup and swing the other leg over..." He lifted her by the waist and she slid right onto the saddle. "There you go."

"Oh!" Noelle laughed with an unexpected surge of joy. "I'm up and ready to roll. Slowly, Rosie. Very, very slowly."

Jace laughed, stepping back to admire her. "You look like a natural. Want me to take a picture and you can post it and shock all your New York buddies?"

"I don't care about them," she said softly, and so

honestly. "I'm just going to be in this moment and not think about anything but Rosie and..." *You.* "And how much fun this is."

His smile lit up his whole face. "That's my girl."

If only she was, Noelle thought as she adjusted herself in the saddle, feeling stiff and unnatural as Rosie took a step.

"Whoa, whoa. I didn't give you permission to move, Rosie."

He chuckled as he climbed up into Jasper's saddle, making it in one smooth move like a literal cowboy. "Remember, she's not a car, she's a creature. She has feelings and thoughts and desires, like we all do."

Desires? She squeezed the reins tighter. "Desires... like to bolt across the mountains and leave me hanging on for dear life?"

He laughed. "No, desires to make you happy, and she can feel if your legs are squeezing with raw fear, so, first thing...relax. Breathe. Let your body go loose."

She followed the instructions, wondering if he knew how difficult it was to do any of those things around him, let alone while atop a thousand-pound animal.

"Now, let me show you the basic commands and how to handle the reins."

By the time he got through a quick lesson, Noelle really did begin to relax.

Once she felt comfortable enough, he guided her out of the pasture and they started along the path that led through Sonny's farm. Rosie was slow and gentle in her steps, as if she knew Noelle was a first-timer and wanted to make it easy.

"How we feelin'?" Jace looked back as they clomped over the wooden red bridge, the sun glinting in her eyes.

"We're great!" Noelle exclaimed. "I love her. We're just taking it slow and easy, cruising through the—"

Rosie stopped suddenly, shaking her head rapidly.

"Oh, boy. What's she doing? Ready to take off?"

"It's okay," Jace said on a laugh. "Something just bothered her. Probably a fly. She's alive, remember?"

"Right." Noelle took a deep breath, leaning forward to pat Rosie's muscular neck. "No more flies, please, Rosie. No more random shakes."

"They can sense fear, you know," Jace called back. "You're calm, the horse will be calm. You're scared, the horse will be scared."

"I am not scared," Noelle insisted, hoping Rosie would get the message. "We're just so relaxed, having a grand old time, just me and my Rosie."

Jace cracked up, his shoulders moving with a laugh as he led the way to a narrow path through the trees into the mountains.

As the horses strolled, it was impossible not to relax into the rhythm of their slow trot, with achingly beautiful mountain views and the scent of the forest around them. As promised, the weather had warmed, melting most of the snow and giving them a picture-perfect Blue Ridge day.

"I forgot how gorgeous it is out here," she said as the path widened and they were able to walk side by side.

"I never take it for granted," he said. "Every morning, I wake up and thank God I live in the shadow of Copper Creek Mountain."

As the sensation of riding began to become second nature, they talked about how the town had changed and become such a draw for tourists, artists, and foodies, but how simple it still was out here, west of Asheville.

"This place sure enchanted my aunt," Noelle said. "Or, I guess, Sonny did."

He nodded. "We've all had so much fun watching those two fall in love. It's been great to have a front-row seat."

She eyed him, thinking of how Hannah had said the same thing, and wondering why Jace didn't take the spunky schoolteacher for rides on horses. "Hannah said that, too," she mused. "She's a sweetheart, don't you think?"

"She's a good kid."

"She's not that much younger than you," she added. "Thirty-three and...still single. She's quite a catch."

He threw her a look, not at all fooled by her less-than-graceful question. "She is, for the right guy, but that guy is not Keith Kelly. And for the record, Hannah and Caro are like sisters to me, and were very close to my wife, since I've been working for Sonny from the day I got my vet degree."

She wanted so much to ask more about his wife, but wasn't sure if that was the right direction to take this conversation. She didn't want to bring him down on such a beautiful day.

"So, the seventeenth floor of a high-rise, huh?" he asked. "That's where I've always imagined you."

"You...imagined me?"

"I looked up your Facebook page a few years ago," he admitted. "But you don't put up much other than comments about art and gallery openings."

Without realizing it, she pulled back on the reins a little, slowing Rosie down so she could give Jace a hard look. "You stalked my Facebook page?"

"I looked up an old friend," he countered with a self-conscious laugh. "Guess that means you never looked me up."

"No, I'm sorry. It's not like I forgot you, but...life moved on."

He nodded, his expression growing serious. "I guess you always associated me—or the memory of me—with the worst thing that ever happened to you."

"That might be true," she whispered. "And I'm sorry, I really am. Part of me felt like I had to wipe every memory from that awful week. Sadly, you were part of a pretty dark time in my life."

He was quiet for a moment, only the sound of hoof-beats as Noelle bounced quietly, pondering what he'd said earlier.

"Was that the reason for that great unraveling you mentioned?" she finally asked.

He nodded slowly. "I took your leaving pretty hard. Tenth-grade drama and all."

"If it's any consolation, Jace...I, uh, I thought about

you a lot. But everything was so uncertain and confusing to me then."

"You think that's the real reason you've stayed single?" he asked. "Fear of losing someone you love again?"

She gave him a surprised look at the uber-personal question.

"Jasper told me to ask," he said quickly. "As your therapist."

She couldn't help a startled burst of laughter. "Well, since my therapist is asking, I can say...maybe. Any connection, of any kind, with the exception of my sisters and aunt, has always been terrifying to me. I stopped trusting...everything." She thought for a minute, then added, "I guess I compensated for that by telling myself that my life is very full and successful, and looking at my wonderful aunt for inspiration...or I used to."

"Wonderful inspirations can change," he said, holding her gaze. "Love is a pretty powerful thing, Noelle, and it can transform a life and priorities, as you can see from Bitsy."

She stared back at him, no doubt in what he was saying, but plenty of doubt as to why he was saying it. Friendly conversation or was he...trying to tell her something? Did he want her to change and become the next...*Bitsy?*

"I suppose it can," she said. "I haven't ever felt love like that, though."

"That's a shame." Jace shrugged, his broad shoulders lifting as he swayed with the movement of the horse.

"I assume you have?" she asked.

"Oh, yeah. Jenny was...amazing. We met when I was about to go to vet school and did the long-distance thing because she was here in Asheville. I honestly don't think we had ten arguments in fifteen years. We were deeply connected and..." His voice trailed off.

"I'm so sorry," she said, feeling like the words had to sound hollow.

But he smiled as if her sympathy touched him. "Yeah, it was a good marriage. I'm sorry you haven't had that kind of love."

Noelle swallowed, unable to deny the ache in her heart or the confusion in her mind. "I'm fulfilled, I'm content on my own. I know people might think I'm just saying that, but I am."

"I believe you," he said with a soft laugh. "Now, come on. Give Rosie a kick and let's get around the next bend. I have a surprise for you."

She frowned, looking around and realizing they weren't far from the widest part of the creek, where they used to fish and...where he'd asked her to be his girlfriend and they had that last kiss on the deck of an abandoned shack.

"What kind of surprise?"

"Honey, if I told you, it wouldn't be a surprise."

As the horses came around a clearing, Noelle sucked in a soft breath, not only awash with memories but also a little bit of shock.

"Is that...the old shack?" She blinked at the tiny structure, which was in the same place as what was once a fishing cottage, and about the same size as what she remembered, but someone had renovated it with love. The weathered brown clapboard was painted white, with black shutters, and the deck had been expanded and now jutted over the creek.

"Turned out, it was on the edge of my property," he said. "My house is about half a mile from here, and this was part of the land, so I spiffed the place up." He gave a dry laugh. "And, yes, I built the deck out far enough so I could throw a line right off the side if the spirit moved me. And move me it does, in the summer. Cassie and I fish out here every weekend from June to September."

"Jace! It's adorable."

"Come on, I'll show you around, though there's not much to see. One room, a bathroom, what could be called a kitchen if you stretch it, and a lot of tackle boxes and such."

Jace rode his horse over to the wooden fence that ran along the side of the creek and climbed off, tying a rope to the fence so Jasper couldn't run away.

Noelle followed on Rosie, and Jace took her reins and then helped her down from the saddle.

He secured her horse, then took a black bag off of Jasper's saddle, swinging it onto his back.

"What's that?" she asked.

"Part of the surprise." He slid into a wide grin. "You don't like surprises, do you?"

She just lifted a shoulder and looked around. "Well, this one's okay. Lots of memories, too." She looked up at him, narrowing her eyes. "Is that why you brought me here?"

"Yep."

"Not playing games, I see."

He started to walk to the shack, then slowed his step and looked right at her. "I learned the hard way that life's too short for games, Noelle. I got you back for, what? A month? I'm fixin' to get the most I can out of it."

Her heart tumbled around her chest. "What does that mean?"

"It means..." He huffed out a breath. "I never *stopped* liking you, Noelle. No, you weren't on my mind all these years, and I had a very happy marriage. Incredibly happy until it was nothing but loneliness and heartache and a kid who was smarter than me when she was two."

She bit her lip, imagining how hard it had to have been.

"And, like you after your parents died, I went a long time thinking that I never wanted to love anyone that much again because it hurts too much to say goodbye. But...I healed. Cassie helped, I'm not gonna lie. But I healed."

She nodded, still not quite sure where he was going with this. "It's inspiring to see that," she said.

"And when the clouds of grief finally lifted," he continued, "I realized that shutting the world out, shutting love out, was not in any way what I was called to do. Jenny would never want that for me, and definitely not for Cassie."

She swayed a little, as though she were still on top of that horse and feeling unsteady. "What exactly are you saying, Jace?"

"That I want to spend as much time with you as I can while you're here. No strings, no expectations, no big future plans. Just old friends who always liked each other a lot."

He reached for her hand to make his point, quiet for a moment as she realized she was holding her breath.

"Look, I know you're going back to New York at the end of the holidays, and that's fine. But for now? For this magical season of happiness and gift-giving and goodwill to man?" He gave her hand a squeeze. "I'm hoping you'll relax and we can just enjoy each other's company. It's the nicest thing that's happened to me in a long time."

For a whole lot of heartbeats, she stared at him, silent and stunned. That speech? Well, it was the nicest thing that had happened to her in a long time, too. No wonder she'd never really dated. Guys like Jace didn't exist in New York. Maybe not anywhere.

"I don't know how I can say no to that," she finally whispered.

"Just in case you were considering it, I have this." He lifted the bag and gave her a sly smile. "Peanut butter and Fluff sandwiches. Not as good as your mom made, but they should bring back some memories. We can eat inside. Come on."

Remembering how her mom always sent her off fishing with Jace stocked with PB&Fs, as she called them, Noelle followed him into the little shack, which was surprisingly bright inside. She sat at one of the few pieces of furniture—a table for four—and let him unpack his sweet surprise, which included a Thermos of hot chocolate.

They ate the sandwiches and talked about...everything. How he met Jenny, what it was like when they had Cassie, how he'd built his vet business from the ground up. She told him about her life in New York, her clients and friends, and how she'd clung to her independence, inspired by her aunt.

By the time they packed up and walked back to the horses, Noelle was beyond relaxed, completely satisfied, and not the least bit nervous about him.

As she passed Jasper, she stroked the horse's mane and added an impulsive kiss. "Good work, therapy horse. I've never felt better."

Laughing, Jace helped her up to the saddle and they rode back together in the most comfortable quiet she could remember since the last time they walked this path together, innocent fifteen-year-olds with a crush on each other.

Now they were forty...and the crush was still there.

Chapter Fourteen

Eve

"Is this for real?" James asked with wild enthusiasm when he caught sight of Sonny's showstopper of a vintage pickup truck parked in front of the house at Red Bridge Farm, ready for a late afternoon Christmas tree cutting. "What kind of truck is it?"

Sonny held the gate of the flatbed open to let them climb into the back where Lucky and a pile of blankets waited for the family.

"She's a 1950 Chevrolet 3100 pickup," he told them. "My daddy bought it used in 1960, if you can believe that. Handed her down and I've been refurbishing it forever. She just had a candy apple paint job and the seats are new, too."

"Are there seatbelts back here?" Bradley asked as he hoisted himself up and checked out the open area. "Or are we just...loose?"

"Lucky doesn't fly out, so you won't, either," Sonny promised him on a chuckle. "I won't go fast up the mountain, and on the way home, y'all will need to hold the tree we're cutting down."

"Where's the axe?" Sawyer asked, already scrambling over the side to get next to the dog, who wagged his tail happily at the sight of his buddy. "Can't cut a tree without an axe!"

"We'll use a battery-powered saw, son, and we'll cut that tree."

Eve smiled up at David as they stood arm in arm, watching.

"True to form, each of them," he murmured. "Curious, worried, and wild."

Sighing, she gave his waist a hug and leaned her head on his shoulder, letting the pure perfection of the moment roll over her. They were a family—solid, happy, and loving—surrounded by her sisters and aunt, everyone connected and close.

"Does it get any better than this?" Aunt Elizabeth whispered, sidling up to Eve.

"I was just thinking that," Eve said. "And the answer is no."

For a split second, they shared a silent look and Elizabeth lifted a brow, leaning in to whisper, "Well, yes, they could be here. But you know what? They are watching from above, smiling from their mansion in heaven, delighted right down to their bones that we're all here together."

Eve studied her. "Really? You think?"

"I don't think, I know. You'll see—you feel it, too."

"What do you mean?"

She lifted a shoulder. "Jackie's all over this mountain, and it used to be the reason I stayed away," she said.

"Now it's the reason I want to be here. I feel her spirit in the air and it makes me miss her less."

"Let's go, lollygaggers!" Sonny gestured them to the truck. "Not you, Bitsy. You are my co-pilot, darlin'."

"I'm on it, Captain!" She slipped away, leaving Eve to hold her last words in her heart then climb into the back, where she and David settled into the only empty space.

Noelle and Angie leaned against the side, handing out wool blankets. It was late enough in the day that the sun was dropping behind the mountains, leaving the air chilled and rich with the scent of pines and earth.

"You warm enough?" David asked as he tucked a checkered blanket around Eve's legs, his face close enough that he could have easily kissed her. And looked like he really wanted to, but out of deference to the boys, he didn't.

"I'm perfect," she said, reaching up to touch his cheek.

"You can say that again." He inched closer, losing the battle and planting a light kiss on her lips. "I love—"

"No seatbelts!" Sawyer dove and splayed his body over their laps, making them both grunt noisily. "What a country!"

They all laughed as Sonny revved a noisy engine, honked the horn, and rolled off to head up the winding road and hairpin turns that would take them to the summit, where he said the best Fraser firs grew for the sole purpose of becoming a family Christmas tree.

"Woo!" Sawyer threw his hands in the air, as if he

were on a roller coaster and not in a truck going about twelve miles per hour.

"Easy, boy," David said, guiding Sawyer back to the side as they turned a corner. "You need to hold on to your dog there, and be still."

"I can't be still!" he announced.

"Truer words were never spoken," Noelle teased, fighting a smile that was impossible not to wear around this kid.

"Watch for bears," Angie reminded him, which instantly did the trick. "They come out at sunset."

"Really?" His eyes widened. "Is that true, James?"

James snorted and threw an arm around Bradley, not saying anything but still oozing that kind protection he always showed to his wary younger brother.

Once again, Eve's heart hitched as she shared a look with David, who'd noticed, too.

"We have great kids," he whispered. "Have I mentioned that?"

"Frequently, but you're not wrong."

"I just...I don't know," he added, sounding wistful.

"What don't you know?" Eve asked.

He cuddled closer, the conversation private as Angie talked to Noelle about her new volunteer position and the boys got noisier with each passing mile.

"I don't know if we should be...you know. Done."

She inched back, eyes widening. "Done...with what?"

He tipped his head toward the boys. "Sometimes I dream there could be one more."

Another baby? Eve sat up a little straighter. Her body

language and shocked expression must have been as loud as the screaming in her head, since it brought Angie and Noelle's conversation to a halt.

"Everything okay over there?" Angie asked.

For a second, Eve was too speechless to answer, but knew instantly this was not the time or place to discuss what he'd just suggested.

"We're great," she said. "The elevation has made my husband lose his mind."

He laughed at that, and so did the others—probably for different reasons—as Sonny chugged the truck higher and higher, until the road flattened out and led them toward a thickly forested area that looked extremely familiar.

"Wait, we've been here before," Angie said, looking around.

"Isn't this where the pond is?" Eve asked, a glimmer of recognition flashing as she took in the surroundings.

"Where we went ice skating!" Angie practically clapped. "Remember that year it froze?"

"Can we ice skate *on a pond?*" Sawyer looked like he might climb out of his skin, or the truck, at the idea.

"No," Eve said quickly. "That was a weird year and it wouldn't be safe now."

"No way I'm ice skating on a pond," Bradley added in his most serious voice. "I can't believe you did it, Mom."

"Well, it was super cold that year and it was..." She felt a smile pull as she looked at her sisters, who no doubt remembered the glorious day—and the frigid winter—

when Mom and Dad brought them up here to skate. "Fun," she finished.

The conversation ended when Sonny pulled into a clearing blanketed in snow, surrounded by acres of Christmas pines. He honked noisily to announce they'd arrived at the community farm where locals were allowed to cut trees in the winter if they supported regrowth in the spring.

"Wow!" James gasped, leaning over the side of the truck bed. "There's, like, a million Christmas trees here!"

"I know!" Bradley agreed, his eyes glinting with joy. "How are we going to pick just one?"

"We'll pick the perfect one," Angie added with a smile. "I trust that you boys will be able to find the best of the best?"

"Oh, yes." James nodded confidently. "Leave it to us."

Eve glanced at David, who was beaming at his sons.

Had he been serious about another child? She was forty, or very nearly so—could she conceive easily? Could her body manage nine more months of pregnancy? And after that, could she handle a newborn? An infant? Diapers and cribs and teething and first steps and...and... oh. Just thinking about it gave her a shiver of longing. She didn't know what she was capable of at forty, but the very idea of a baby did fill her with an overwhelming longing to have one more.

Was maternal instinct that strong that it could override...*common sense*? He was never home! How could she possibly—

"We have arrived!" Aunt Elizabeth sang as she

climbed out to stomp her boots on the snow-covered ground, her newfound joy so palpable that Eve still couldn't get used to it.

"Okay, boys." Eve clapped her hands, snapping herself out of her baby thoughts and back to the present moment with the three sons she already had.

But, oh. A...*girl.*

"Out we go, men." David rose to pick up the slack, since Eve was obviously too stunned to move. "And dog," he added, letting Lucky leap out as Sonny unlatched the tailgate.

After the boys shot out and started running around, the others followed, getting their bearings and checking out the winter white beauty of the tree farm. There were a few other families out here on the same mission, but for the most part, they had the place to themselves.

"Can anyone take these trees down, Uncle Sonny?" James asked.

As he explained the workings of the community farm, Eve relished the crunch of the snow underneath her boots as she tried to keep track of each of her sons, all shooting off in different directions.

"Relax," David said, wrapping an arm around her. "They're with Sonny and Angie and Noelle. Enjoy the moment alone."

"Says the man who just suggested...a *fourth.*"

He chuckled, but didn't deny a thing. Didn't make a joke or assure her that the moment of madness had passed. On the contrary, he looked hard at her, the light of dusk revealing the spark of hope in his hazel eyes.

"Would it be the worst thing in the world?" he asked quietly, easily guiding her to a grouping of fir trees.

"On a week when you work sixty hours, homeschool test scores are due, and I have to be at a soccer game, swim practice, and a meeting for the play parents all at the same time? Yes."

He made a face, looking both disappointed and understanding. "Yeah, that's...too much."

She took a breath and looked up at him. "That said? I don't hate the idea."

"Really? What if it's a boy?"

"I love boys," she said without a second's hesitation. "And I have all the clothes, toys, and gear. But, honey..." She shook her head. "I can't do it without you."

He looked away for a beat, his gaze on the mountains, his head...somewhere else. She knew David well enough to know when those wheels were turning, solving problems, thinking through all the options, making the right decisions.

"I'd cut back at work."

"Really? You can just do that?" Then why didn't he?

"It probably would mean I won't be a partner in the practice."

She frowned. "You've wanted that promotion for a long time, David. Are you sure you want to give it up?"

"It just means more meetings, more admin, more time away. And more money," he added. "But we're in a solid position."

She rubbed her arms as a chilly breeze rustled the

pine needles around them. "I can't believe we're having this conversation," she said. "What brought it on?"

"You. The boys. Being here. I don't know. I love this solid family feeling and we make such incredible little humans, Eve. I just..." His voice cracked. "I love you so much and I love them and sometimes I wish we had another child. That's the best part of my life, and that's the God's truth."

She smiled up at him, knowing that it was. David was nothing if not one hundred percent authentic.

The boys' laughter and voices floated over to them, pulling her attention. "They are having the most awesome Christmas season ever," she said. "I'm so grateful we're here."

"David!" Aunt Elizabeth called. "You need to break a tie on the choice of tree!"

"Be right there." He pulled her into him and gave her a light kiss. "Just think about it. See if it feels right or...nuts."

"Can it feel both?"

He laughed and nodded, jogging toward their family's voices, leaving Eve to stand very still in the waning light for a long time, thinking about the impractical, incredible, and slightly dreamy possibility of having another child.

"Come and see the tree, Mommy!" Sawyer danced around her with Lucky right on his heels as he dragged her toward the rest of the group. "I found it. Well, me and Lucky did."

"Lucky and I," she corrected, the homeschooler in her never really on vacation.

"No, you were talking to Daddy," he said, too wrapped up in Christmas joy to have his grammar corrected. Eve reached down and scooped up her baby, lifting him off the ground and giving him an unexpected kiss.

He squirmed, but accepted his fate. "You're gonna love the tree!" he said on a half-giggle.

"I love you," she countered, kissing some more.

It was too much for him, as he squiggled free and shot off to where Sonny and Elizabeth stood admiring a tall Fraser fir.

Giving up her search for affection—could a girl be better at that?—she joined the gang. "Is it true?" she asked. "Have we located our most special Christmas tree?"

Sonny gave a big thumbs-up and a huge smile. "We sure did. She's a beauty, perched on the back edge of the farm."

"I found it first!" James asserted, raising his hand.

"Did not!" Sawyer crossed his arms. "I saw it as soon as we got here."

"No, you didn't," James insisted.

Bradley stepped forward. "We all found it together."

"That's right," she agreed, reaching for her darling

middle child to hold him close to her. "So what are we doing here? Let's get it."

Sonny let out a hearty chuckle. "Well, years ago I'd have done it myself, of course. But age has brought me some back problems, and I don't wanna be hurtin' on the holidays, so I'm waiting on some backup."

"Hey, everyone." The unfamiliar male voice called to them from the road and they all turned to see a man striding toward them in a red flannel shirt, a down vest, and jeans, with what looked like an electric saw in one hand. But in the other, he held the hand of a little girl who trudged through the snow with purpose and power.

And suddenly Eve knew who this man was. She turned to look at Noelle's reaction, in time to see Angie doing the same thing. They both caught their sister brighten and tuck her hair behind her ears in an extremely out-of-character moment of self-consciousness.

Well, what do you know? Noelle really did like Jace Fleming...*again.*

"Nice to meet you all." Jace shook hands and acquainted himself with the whole group, even crouching down to give high-fives to her little boys, which was sweet. "This is my daughter, Cassie."

"Hi!" Cassie, an outgoing little thing, marched right up to Noelle. "Remember me?"

"You're unforgettable," Noelle replied, bending over. "Where's Sprinkles?"

"Home at the ranch. Do you want to come and visit her soon? Tomorrow? You could walk her with me."

"Easy, Cass." Jace put his hand on the little girl's

shoulder and smiled at Noelle. "She'll have you doing chores with her if you're not careful."

"I wouldn't hate that," she responded, unable to wipe the smile from her face as she looked at him.

Eve inched forward to look past them and catch Angie's gaze. She met Eve's eyes and they gave each other the "do you see what I see" look.

"And I'll be happy to take Sprinkles the goat for a walk," Noelle added, giving Cassie's hair a ruffle to break the moment.

"You walk a goat?" Bradley moved closer. "Like, with a leash? That's cool!"

"Mm-hmm!" She nodded proudly. "We keep all sorts of animals at the ranch. I can show you sometime."

"I hear there's a Christmas tree that needs to be cut." Jace lifted his chainsaw. "Have we picked one out yet?"

"Yes!" Sawyer answered first, waving him toward the tree. "It's right over there, the most perfect Christmas tree in the whole wide world."

"In the whole wide world?" Jace gave a soft hoot. "Well, aren't we the lucky ones."

"Follow me!" Sawyer took off running through the trees and Jace stayed close behind him, with Cassie, Bradley, and James—and Lucky—trailing after them.

"Let's go," Sonny said, putting a hand on David's shoulder. "Otherwise your son will be working that chainsaw."

"Oh, no, he won't."

The two men took off, leaving Eve, Noelle, Angie, and Elizabeth in a group.

"Let's go look at the pond," Elizabeth murmured. "I want to see if I remember skating there, too."

"Yeah, and can we talk about Jace?" Angie grabbed Noelle's arm and pulled her closer. "Cute with a capital Q."

Noelle rolled her eyes at that and shrugged. "He's a sweetie, no doubt about it."

Eve stepped closer. "The man has aged exceptionally well, I must agree. Not to mention the way he looked at you."

Noelle gave a pleading look to their aunt. "Make them stop, Aunt *Bitsy*," she whined playfully, getting a laugh from all of them.

"I can't," Elizabeth said. "I'm too thrilled with the possibility."

"There's no possibility," Noelle countered. "We're old friends who will probably spend a bit of time together while I'm here this month. Then it's wheels up and back to the city, where I belong."

"Why couldn't it be something more?" Eve asked. "I mean, the chemistry is palpable."

"Electrical," Angie agreed. "Sparks were flying."

"I think you were looking at the chainsaw," Noelle said, throwing her a look. "Guys, you're all very cute, but Jace is a widower and single dad who lives on a ranch in North Carolina. I am a successful art dealer who works sixty hours a week for Sotheby's. Oil and water and you're wasting your time. A relationship with him is impossible."

Aunt Elizabeth stepped into the fray, putting her arm around Noelle. "Um, Noelle, darling?"

Noelle gave her a wary look. "Please be on my side," she whispered. "Please."

"I'm on the side of happiness and complete hearts," she said. "And if I've learned anything from my time with a widower and single dad who lives on a farm in North Carolina, it's something straight out of my favorite book."

"What's that?" Noelle asked.

"Nothing is impossible with God." At their looks, she held up her hand to silence them. "I am simply saying that you think you have a plan and a path, and it just might not be the one He has set out for you."

None of them said a word, no doubt for all different reasons. Noelle was probably holding back more denials and Angie was likely thinking about her own marriage and how it wasn't going as she'd planned.

But as they stepped toward an embankment and looked out over the last of the daylight reflected on the water of a pond that held her best and dearest memories, Eve thought about...another baby.

Nothing was impossible with God. Maybe He knew what she should do, and maybe He'd give her a sign.

"This is the place," Angie said on a reverent whisper. "We came, we saw, and, man, we skated."

"*You* skated," Noelle cracked. "I fell on my butt a thousand times."

Eve smiled at the memory, spotting something bright moving in the trees. "What is that?"

"A cardinal," Elizabeth said. "They're all over here

this time of year, collecting branches and twigs for the nests they'll need in the spring. That's when they'll lay eggs and bring more beautiful birds to the land."

They shifted their gazes to where a single red bird fluttered on the branch of a tree, then took off, swooping over the water, and back to another tree.

Was that her sign that she should bring...more beautiful birds to the land?

Suddenly, they heard a hum in the distance, a high-pitched whine and some delighted screams from the kids.

"We did it! We did it!" Sawyer's voice carried through the forest, wild with excitement. "We cut down our tree!"

They all shared a smile and a hug, then headed back to the group. As they walked, Eve took one more look over her shoulder, searching for the cardinal, but it was gone.

Chapter Fifteen

Noelle

NOELLE ROSE WITH THE SUN, feeling far from New York and work and all the responsibilities that used to matter. Instead of thinking about the upcoming auction or the email Lucinda Butler had sent ordering her to find a very specific piece for the next gallery opening in Soho, she was thinking about a man and his chainsaw and his precious little girl.

The cabin was silent and still at this hour, and she tiptoed downstairs and made coffee as quietly as possible. They'd stayed up late again, sipping on Irish whiskey, sharing thoughts and sisterly conversation.

But both of her sisters seemed a little all over the place. Eve was sad that David would be leaving this morning, but he'd be back for the tree lighting on Saturday in town. Angie was over the moon that she'd be starting her volunteer work at Biltmore House soon, but confessed that she hadn't talked to Craig in many days.

Which only made Noelle wonder...*were you ever really safe loving someone?*

Mug in hand, Noelle curled up on a wicker rocking

chair in the sunroom, gently swaying. She had a few pesky thoughts about her laptop and phone being upstairs, but for the first time in forever, she didn't care about emails or phone calls or big fat deals.

Instead she wanted to think about peanut butter and Fluff sandwiches and a man who said the sweetest things and seemed to have no problem letting her know he was interested. *Oh, Jace.* He did need love, and she was sure he'd find it again—and make some kind country girl incredibly happy.

Noelle shut her eyes, and for the tiniest, most fleeting moment, she thought about what it would be like to be that country girl. To have that slow, easy life with him and to be a mom to little Cassie.

She'd never be a mother now; that ship had sailed. But there was Cassie...just stealing Noelle's heart and making her imagine things she'd long ago taken off her list of possible life roads.

The sound of a vehicle engine surprised her at this hour, making her head back inside to look toward the front and see Sonny's iconic red truck rolling up the driveway.

Stepping out to the porch with her coffee, she offered a friendly wave as he parked and climbed out. She wasn't exactly in the mood to chat, but the fact was she still hadn't had a one-on-one conversation with him. She'd promised Aunt Elizabeth she'd make an effort to get to know the man, and this was her golden opportunity.

"You're up early, Noelle," he called.

"And I made coffee. Would you like some?"

"You bet I would. I'll need it for the work ahead."

"Work?" she asked.

"I'm fixin' to get the outdoor lights up. Bitsy was fussin' last night about how much she wants every gable and window trimmed and..." He angled his head with mock shame. "I simply can't say no to the woman. Have you noticed?"

"I have and it's sweet."

"Well..." He walked toward the front steps and added a warm smile. "Would you mind company with that coffee or are you clicking away on your computer already?"

"I'm just enjoying the sunroom," she said. "And you're more than welcome to join me." Maybe she'd get to know what made the man tick, and what kind of magic dust he'd sprinkled over Aunt Elizabeth to change her so much.

With fresh coffee poured, they settled in the wicker chairs, making small talk about the view and the sunrise, and how this room was such a great addition to the house. Every word he said was slow and easy, as Southern as sweet tea.

Was that what Elizabeth had seen in him? She had been, after all, a North Carolina girl long before she was a world-traveling jetsetter. Maybe he took her back to her roots.

Was that enough to make the world's most independent woman uproot her entire life and adopt a new look and attitude?

"So, Noelle," Sonny said slowly, pressing his hands to

the tops of his faded jeans like he was maybe a little bit nervous. "I knew you were gonna be a tough nut to crack. And believe me, I get it. You and Bitsy went together like biscuits and gravy, and now she's a totally different woman and you hardly recognize her."

"Oh, I recognize her," she said. "I'm surprised, is all. I guess I want to be sure this transformation is right for her, and won't leave her...hurt when it ends."

"Who said anything about it ending?"

She lifted a shoulder. "Breakups happen."

He snorted as if she'd suggested the moon would fall from the sky. "Her transformation, as you call it, didn't happen overnight, you know. And the change is so good."

That was debatable. "She feels like an entirely different person."

"In some ways, she is; in others, she isn't," he said. "The woman I fell in love with was sassy, and fun, and she still can make me laugh at anything. She was also so capable, and never wanted to ask for help with anything." He added a look. "Heck, if she wanted to, she'd hang the dang lights on the roof herself. I just won't let her."

"That was her." Noelle shrugged and gave a dry laugh. "That's how she used to be."

"That's who she still is, Noelle." He locked eyes with her, and his expression was nothing but earnest and sincere. "She's changed her priorities and her lifestyle, not her fundamental personality. She's still the incredible woman who made you who you are. I'd argue she's even more incredible now."

Noelle ran a hand through her hair, sighing into a sip of coffee as she considered his words.

"And look," he continued. "I know you've got your reservations about me, and I respect the heck outta you for how much you care for Bitsy. You just want to protect her, and I get that."

She watched him, waiting for the rest.

"I am here to tell you the honest to God truth, honey. I never thought I could love again after my wife died. I never dreamed..." His voice grew thick with emotion. "I thought a man only gets that kind of love once in his lifetime, you know? And then..." He closed his eyes as if he were fighting tears. "She appeared like an angel from God. I felt Him tap my shoulder that day in the antiques store, and nudge me toward her. I really did. I could hear His voice—not actually in my ear, but in my soul—telling me He had one fine surprise for me and that my lonely days were over."

She stared at him, her heart hammering as she thought of...Jace. How could she not?

"And, no, she wasn't what I expected would catch my eye, and I sure wasn't the kind of man she'd ever give a second look to." He gave a rumble of a laugh that came from deep in his chest. "But she was open and interested, and I think...well, don't take this as prideful, because it's not, but I think God wanted me to help bring her to Him. And as a reward for opening her heart to His love, God gave me hers."

He turned to her, his eyes misty, his cheeks a little

bright with emotion, the power of it leaving Noelle speechless.

"I'm here to tell you that I am head over heels in love with your Aunt Elizabeth, and there is no agenda or hidden intentions in my heart. I adore every last little thing about that woman, and I mean to spend the rest of my life making sure she knows it. I want nothing to do with money or riches or bank accounts, that I promise you. My farm has sustained my family for two generations, and that's how it's gonna stay. I love her, Noelle. And she loves me, too. That much is certain."

Noelle met Sonny's warm gaze, feeling her heart shift and soften.

"Sonny, I..." She put her cup on the table as she closed her eyes and attempted to gather her emotions and her words. All she could feel was...shame. "I'm so sorry I doubted you."

He held up a hand. "Don't apologize. You had every right."

"No, I should have had a more open heart and mind. I should have been thrilled about the fact that she's so happy." She shook her head, the truth suddenly becoming so clear. "It was selfish of me to assume there was something wrong or dishonest about your relationship without even giving it a fair chance. I'm sorry."

Sonny's smile was as bright as the sun peeking over the mountains. "You may have inherited your auntie's passion and ambition and independence, but you also inherited that big ole heart of hers. And that's going to serve you well."

Noelle laughed as relief lifted weight off of her shoulders. "Thanks."

He raised his brows. "For the record, I never set out to change her. That just happened, like miracles do. God changed her. Love changed her. I just happened to be in the right place at the right time."

Noelle inhaled slowly, rocking back and forth in her chair, her whole being lighter and...curious. What would it be like to experience that kind of love and change? She ached with the wonder of how a person could just reinvent her whole life.

"Truthfully, I've never seen her so...happy," Noelle mused. "She's got this kind of radiant peace about her that's coming from within."

Sonny nodded. "She sure does. And if there ever comes a day when you want to change up your whole life, she should serve as a reminder that it can be done."

Noelle blew out a long sigh. "Wouldn't be the first time Elizabeth Whitaker taught me a life lesson."

"Amen to that, young lady. Now, you want to help hang some Christmas lights?"

She looked up at him, so happy he'd stopped by, and for the first time since she'd arrived, she felt wholly at peace with him. "I sure do."

HALF AN HOUR LATER, Noelle stood next to Sonny in the front yard, the two of them staring straight up at the roofline.

"All the way up there?" she asked, pointing at the highest gable on the roof, over the third floor. "We never hung lights up there when we were kids, even on my dad's most ambitious days."

"Well, Bitsy wants 'em," he said. "And what I want is an extension pole, 'cause I could do it if I had one."

The ladder he'd brought out of the garage didn't even come close to the distance they needed.

"In the garage or attic, you think?" she asked, ready to get it for him.

He shook his head. "No, but Jace has one at the ranch. I can run over and grab it from him before he starts out on calls."

"I can go," Noelle said, hoping she didn't sound...too eager. "I mean, you can do the lower stuff while I go. No reason to lose all that time."

"Would ya?" Sonny smiled in a way that made her think he already knew she'd offer. "That'd be so helpful. You're right, I can do the first floor and when those boys get out here, I'll put them to work on the railings. We can knock out a big piece of this today."

"Sure." Noelle shrugged casually. "I wouldn't mind a drive. I can borrow Eve's van."

"Here ya go." He reached into the pocket of his jeans and flipped her a set of keys. "Take my truck. More fun than a minivan."

"No kidding."

"Go like you're headed to my farm, then stay on that

road. Keep riding on it for about two more miles, and you'll reach Jace's ranch. There's a picket fence in front of a brick house, some sheds and stuff. You'll see his truck."

She had to smile at the "country" directions. Who needed GPS when there were picket fences and some sheds?

"Can do. Be back soon." Noelle headed down the driveway to the truck in all its shiny red 1950s glory.

She felt a lightness in her heart that may or may not have been intensified by the fact that she was about to go see Jace.

"Wow," Noelle whispered to herself as she climbed into Sonny's truck, admiring its flawless and fabulously vintage interior.

After a breezy, beautiful, twelve-minute drive through the mountains, she reached Jace's ranch, which was as easy to find as Sonny had promised.

A long driveway led to a pretty, one-story brick house on a big piece of property with wide-open views.

Noelle parked the truck and climbed out, and heard something that sounded like a goat bleating, which made her certain she was in the right place.

Here goes nothing, Noelle thought to herself as she walked up to the porch, taking a quick second to smooth her hair, realizing she'd dressed in sweats, sneakers, and a thick sweater over a tank top to help Sonny, and wore not one drop of makeup.

Heck, she really *was* Bitsy 2.0.

She knocked a few times, stepping back for a moment

before the door opened to reveal Jace, surprised and gorgeous and...*shirtless*.

"Whoa, Noelle. Hi.".

"I'm so sorry. Did I wake you?"

He glanced down, maybe embarrassed about his lack of clothing. "I've been up a bit. To what do I owe this very pleasant and unexpected visit?"

Noelle smiled, noticing the way his chestnut hair was still a little messy, and how his eyes lit up when he looked at her.

"I need to borrow an extension pole, for hanging lights," she explained. "Sonny and I were getting an early start, and he seems to believe you'd have one."

"I think I can be of service." Jace angled his head, opening the door all the way. "Come on in."

"Great, thank you." Noelle stepped into the house, which was simple and neat and lovely.

She noticed a cozy-looking living room with a tall stone fireplace opposite the kitchen, which had the same country feeling as Sonny's.

Out back there was a large deck and a trampoline, which she bet Cassie loved.

"Let me go grab a shirt," he said with a self-conscious laugh. "Make yourself at home. You want coffee or anything?"

She stole another glance at muscles and skin and willed herself not to stare. "I'm good. You can just...dress."

Chuckling, he disappeared down a hall while she perched on the edge of a chair at the kitchen table, where a half a cup of creamy coffee sat next to an iPad that had gone dark.

She scanned his kitchen, somehow feeling like she'd invaded his privacy, her gaze stopping at the fridge covered in what was clearly Cassie's artwork. Elaborate drawings of every animal under the sun, and they were all hung with magnets and carefully, lovingly displayed.

What an angel Cassie was, and what a good dad she had.

"All right, now that I'm decent." Jace winked as he walked back into the room, having put on a white T-shirt that made him look almost as attractive as when he was shirtless. "Let's get you that extender. But you sure you don't want a cup of coffee first?"

"I've already had two this morning. But I'll take a water." Since the sight of him had left her a little parched. "Unless you're going out on calls. Sonny thought you might be."

"I've got several later this morning," he said, filling a glass with water. When he gave it to her, he sat down across from her, giving her a slightly loopy grin. "Man, I can't actually think of a better way to start my morning than having Noelle Chambers sitting in my kitchen with me."

She laughed, feeling her cheeks warm. "I volunteered to drive over," she admitted with a sly smile. "So..."

He just smiled like she'd handed him a thousand-dollar bill. "So, you and Sonny are becoming pals, huh? Hanging lights together in the early morning?"

"We had a talk," Noelle told him. "A good talk. I

misjudged him, and I was close-minded. I want to give him and their relationship a fair chance, no matter how shocking it may seem."

Jace nodded slowly, listening as his eyes grew warm with appreciation. "That's awesome. I'm really glad you got a chance to spend some time with him. Sonny's a great guy, and those two? The real deal."

Noelle sucked in a breath. "I'm starting to really understand that. I guess the right relationship can change you. Make you reinvent your life, as Sonny put it."

"It sure can." Jace braced his chin on his knuckles and stared at her, the look just intense enough to give her heart a flip.

She already knew what it was like to kiss the boy Jace had been...but what about this man? Would he—

"I didn't know you were here!" Cassie bounded into the kitchen in a pink nightgown with a unicorn and the words "My Little Pony" on it, her hair a complete mess.

Noelle cleared her throat and pulled back, not realizing how close she'd gotten to Jace. "Hi, Cassie. I came over to borrow a tool from your daddy. I hope I didn't wake you up."

"Oh, no. I get up early to take care of the animals."

"It's true," Jace added. "Cassie takes her morning ranch duties very seriously. Never misses a day."

"That's wonderful." Noelle gave the little girl a hug, which seemed like the most natural thing in the world. "That kind of discipline will serve you well in life, no matter what you decide to do."

"Let me go grab you that extender." Jace stood up.

"Of course," Noelle said quickly, suddenly feeling like she might be intruding on their precious morning father-daughter time. "I don't want to keep Sonny waiting."

"Be right back." Jace walked out through a door that led to the garage.

Noelle turned to Cassie. "So, do you have school today?"

"No, it's done for Christmas now, which means I probably go to Grandma's if Daddy has calls for work."

"I think he does," Noelle said.

The little girl made a face. "Then I better get to work," she said, sounding more like an overworked corporate lawyer than a seven-year-old on a farm.

Jace came back in with a nod. "I put it in the back of Sonny's truck," he said.

"Thank you." She stood and took her water glass to the sink.

"Anytime. Tell Sonny that—" He was cut off by the ringing of a phone in his pocket. "That's my emergency line," he said, as if to explain why he was answering. "Hello, this is Dr. Fleming." He waited a beat, then frowned. "Eyes open or closed?" Another beat. "Can you get his temperature? Do your best, keep him calm, and I can be there in twenty minutes, Martin. Hang tight."

"Is everything okay?" Noelle asked when he disconnected.

Jace's brows knit together in concern and stress. "One of Martin Abernathy's goats is having a seizure."

Cassie gasped. "Oh, no!"

"It's okay, sweetie," Jace assured her. "I have the

meds he needs, but I've got to get over there now and try to figure out what caused it. Please get dressed as fast as you can and I'll drive you to Grandma's, but it's in the other direction, so be quick."

"I haven't done my chores, Daddy."

"They can—"

"I'll stay with her," Noelle said, wanting so much to help out with this little family crisis. "Or I can take her to your parents' house."

"Please stay, please!" Cassie practically shouted. "Miss Noelle can help with my chores."

Jace lifted a brow as he braced on the counter and pushed a sock-covered foot into a boot. "I don't think she wants to do that, honey."

"I don't mind," Noelle assured him, having no qualms about spending time with the enchanting little rancher girl. "Go take care of the goat, and I'll hang here with Cassie. If you get delayed, I can drive her to your mother's. It's no problem."

He looked at her with pure gratitude. "That would be so awesome. In fact, I have to pass the cabin on my way to Martin's house, so I'll toss the extender to Sonny and tell him where you are."

"Perfect."

He bent down to lace up the boot, looking up at her. "Are you sure, Noelle? I know you've got a lot going on, and—"

"I'm positive," Noelle insisted, and meant it. "We'll have a grand old time, right, Cassie?"

"Yeah!" Cassie leapt in the air.

"Okay." Jace nodded and bent down to give his daughter a big kiss on the cheek. "Please be good with Miss Noelle. Now go get dressed."

"Bye, Daddy!"

As she zipped away, he finished tying the other boot and straightened, taking a few steps closer to Noelle. "Thank you. I owe you one."

"You don't owe me a thing," she said.

"We can clean the goat poop first, Miss Noelle," Cassie called from down the hall.

Jace looked at her, fighting a smile. "Like I said, I owe you one."

Noelle cracked up. "Yeah, come to think of it, you might."

His blue eyes danced with humor and something else she couldn't quite read but she knew this much—if they stood here staring at each other much longer, there'd be a kiss before long.

Taking a step back as if he realized that, too, he grabbed a ballcap and keys from a hook by the door and hoisted a large bag over his shoulder. "Have fun."

He'd no sooner walked out than Cassie came running back in wearing jeans, a sweater, and boots of her own. "Let's get to chores, Miss Noelle. The goats need us!"

"Just show me what I can help with," Noelle said, following her to the back deck.

"Miss Noelle." Cassie stepped back, looking Noelle up and down with a noticeably critical eye. "Those shoes are really white."

Noelle looked down at her sneakers that somehow

had managed to stay white. "Well, yeah. I had them on in the stables at Sonny's, so it's okay."

"It's different here. Poopier." Cassie clicked her tongue and folded her arms, thinking. "I have an idea." She waved her hand and led Noelle back into the house, where she opened the door to a coat closet in the hall. "You can wear these boots instead."

Noelle looked at the black rubber work boots Cassie pulled out, knowing they were definitely women's shoes.

Did they belong to Jace's late wife? If they did, Cassie didn't seem to mind.

"Oh, are you sure?" Noelle asked.

"Oh, yes." Cassie nodded. "Come on, hurry. The animals are hungry."

Noelle took off her fancy sneakers and slid into the work boots, following Cassie around the back to the boarding pens and houses for animals.

"Right now, we've got three goats, two pigs, and a sheep." Cassie opened the door and marched in.

"Full house," Noelle remarked.

Cassie giggled. "I love it when we have a lot."

"What do we do first?"

"First..." Cassie walked over to the corner of the stable, which was half open to the outside with pens and enclosures for the animals to roam freely. "We scoop."

"Of course we do."

"It's yucky." Cassie handed her a long tool that could only best be described as a pooper scooper. "But you get used to it."

"We'll see about that."

With Cassie the Capable leading the charge, Noelle followed her instructions and began cleaning out the goat pen.

One of the goats walked right up to her, staring at Noelle with giant eyes.

"Oh. Oh, my." Noelle backed up, not entirely sure about this creature. "Hello. You're a friendly one."

Cassie giggled wildly from the next pen over. "That's Melody. She won't hurt ya."

Noelle wasn't convinced, although Melody certainly didn't look vicious. "I don't, uh, have much experience with—whoa!"

Melody lunged forward, pressing her face against Noelle's leg.

"Give her a pet," Cassie said. "She doesn't bite. Usually."

Noelle bent down, hesitantly reaching her hand to the top of the goat's head and giving her a very gentle rub. "Hi, Mel."

She made a very goat-like sound, closed her eyes, and moved closer to Noelle.

"She likes you!" Cassie announced.

Noelle scratched Melody's soft tufts of hair. "Oh, you're not so bad at all."

Once she settled into the task and got past the smells, Noelle actually found herself enjoying working in the animal pens.

After they'd scooped the grounds and fed Melody and Sprinkles, Cassie threw her arms up and smiled big. "Aren't they just the best?"

"I have to admit, this isn't so bad."

Cassie gave a tooth-gapped grin, her sweet face bright and happy in the sunshine. "You're a natural, Miss Noelle."

"Well, I don't know if I would go that far." Noelle laughed off the compliment. "What's next?"

"We milk 'em!" Cassie waved her to a stool and small structure where the goats would stand.

Twenty minutes and several small tin buckets of milk later, Noelle Chambers actually found herself wearing rubber work books with a significant amount of animal waste on them, walking along the property of a farm, holding a goat on a leash.

Maybe Aunt Elizabeth was right. Maybe anything was possible.

As Cassie filled her in on all the fun she was having rehearsing her Nativity play and learning the songs, Noelle couldn't help but take a mental snapshot of this moment.

She wanted to hold on to this little girl, who was too adorable not to love, and her incredible father, who'd captured Noelle's heart twenty-five years ago and maybe never fully given it back. They were quite the pair. And this life was quite...the life.

The goats and the ranch and the town and the mountains...Noelle took a deep breath and tried to bring herself back to reality.

She lived in New York in a high-rise and worked in an amazing office and had the life of her dreams.

Why was she actually pondering what "reinvention"

would look like? Was she seriously thinking and dreaming about this simple little farm life with Jace and his sweet daughter?

No, she reminded herself. She couldn't fall in love with them. She couldn't go down this road.

Aunt Elizabeth may have turned her whole world upside down and changed everything for love, but Noelle was different. It was silly and ridiculous to even think otherwise.

After a long walk, they went back into the house to clean up as Jace walked in.

"Is the goat okay?" Cassie asked anxiously the second she saw her father.

"He's completely fine, honey." Jace let out a sigh of relief and kissed the top of Cassie's head. "We got him all sorted out, don't you worry."

"Whew," Noelle said. "Thank goodness."

Jace drew back at the sight of Noelle, raising his brows in sheer amusement as he looked her up and down, taking in the work boots, manure, and endless dirt. "You've, uh, been busy."

"Oh, I was just helping Cassie with the chores."

Jace nodded, his eyes glued to Noelle. "I see that. You ladies must be hungry then."

"Starving!" Cassie shouted dramatically.

"Come on." Jace nodded toward the kitchen table. "I'll fix us something. Stay, Noelle."

"I promised Sonny—"

"I just went by there. All three boys are helping, with Bitsy supervising and Eve taking pictures. You can go back, sure, but...we'd love if you stayed with us for a while."

There really was no contest. Noelle sat down at the kitchen table with Cassie, looking around at the life she could maybe have if she reinvented hers entirely. She wouldn't, but it was fun to pretend.

Chapter Sixteen

Angie

BY THE END of the week, life at the Asheville cabin had settled into the sweetest new normal, which Angie was really starting to enjoy. Sonny and the boys had finished putting up the outside lights, giving the whole property the perfect Christmas glow after the sun went down.

They'd fallen into the habit of gathering in the sunroom around six each evening, while the boys were upstairs cleaning up for dinner. Most nights, the sisters cooked—meaning Eve was in charge, Angie was her assistant, and Noelle poured the wine—but sometimes, like tonight, Aunt Elizabeth and Sonny did the honors.

That left the three of them to catch each other up on their days, as they were right now, listening to Noelle wax on about Jace. They'd gone to town with Cassie one day, and had dinner last night, and tomorrow they'd be at the tree lighting.

Angie and Eve shared a not-so-secret smile at just how hard their sister had fallen.

"Oh, I know what you two are thinking," Noelle said

on a laugh. "I'm not in love, okay? I've just been feeling a bit of a change in my heart, I guess. It's everything. It's Aunt Elizabeth and Sonny. It's seeing Jace again and getting to know him as an adult, and being back at this cabin. Things feel like they are shifting and I don't know if that's good or bad."

"I think it's good," Eve said, putting a hand on Noelle's lap. "You seem happy."

"I'm having fun with him," Noelle admitted. "But enough about me. You were at Biltmore House all day, Ange. How'd it go?"

"Amazing," she said, thinking about the long day of getting acclimated and meeting other volunteers, curators, and Marjorie's small staff. Her security clearance had come through and she would start the job of cataloging the new "Below Stairs" exhibit on Monday.

"But I spent hours in that room today," she told her sisters, grabbing her phone to show them some pictures. "You know, I've been so obsessed with Angelica, I've given short shrift to poor Garland, our great-grandfather. Here's a picture of Garland next to Edith Vanderbilt, who is Cornelia's mother."

She passed the phone to Eve and Noelle on the sofa, who leaned in to look together.

"Oh, look at him. Bradley has his eyes!" Eve exclaimed.

"Thank goodness he doesn't have his 'stache," Noelle joked. "He could stand to trim that thing."

"I think he's handsome," Eve said, handing the phone

back. "And I think you're happy, Ms. Angel Chambers Messina."

Angie smiled, not about to deny she was happy—at least about her work at Biltmore House. The rest of her life? Not so much, but she didn't want to get into that now.

"I'm happy about this project," she told them, choosing her words carefully so they were completely honest. "I love that house and the history and the people are great. You'll see when we go on the tour later this month."

"Oh, I hope David is here," Eve said.

"He gets back tomorrow, right?" Noelle asked. "For the tree lighting in town?"

"God willing, and he is supposed to stay straight through to New Year's Day, but I'll believe that when I see it." She wrinkled her nose. "I just can't imagine..." Her voice trailed off and she shifted in her seat, not finishing.

"You can't imagine him being here for that long?" Angie asked, curious what she was going to say since she'd made a lot of wistful, incomplete statements like that lately.

"Yeah," she said quickly. "But back to your project. Have you told Craig about it?"

Angie lifted a shoulder as if it was her turn to be vague.

"Have you talked to Craig?" Noelle asked.

"Texted," she said. "You think Dr. David is busy? Try

reaching the VP of Marketing for Atlas Technologies." Angie rolled her eyes. "Or, for that matter, our daughter."

"You haven't talked to Brooke, either?" Eve gave her a concerned look.

Guess there was no way to keep the real truth out of this conversation—her sisters knew and loved her too much. "I have," she said. "Well, texts. She's almost as hard to reach, and..." She looked from one sister to the other, knowing the can of worms this would open, but saying it anyway. "I don't think either one of them even care that I'm here."

"Oh, honey, no." Noelle pressed her hand to her chest. "I doubt that's true. They're just busy."

"No, it's true," she answered. "Not only don't they miss me, I think they'd be perfectly happy if I never came back. I mean, let's be honest, huh? My marriage is a, um... trainwreck." She blinked an unexpected tear. "Wow, didn't want to go there now, but here we are."

Her sisters stared at her but didn't look exactly shocked. Eve knew, of course, and Noelle wasn't blind or dumb no matter how wrapped up in Jace she was.

"What are you going to do about that?" Eve asked gently.

"Bury myself in history?" she joked. "I don't know. I'm definitely trying to ignore the truth and figure it out... next year. That sounds like the plan of a procrastinator, doesn't it?"

"It sounds like someone who should have a heart-to-heart with her husband," Noelle said.

"And your daughter," Eve added.

Angie's eyes shuttered. "Eve, you have three boys who are connected to you, who love and respect you, and who understand what family is. I have a teenager who is obsessed with TikTok and material things and a new boyfriend and she wants nothing—and I do mean *nothing*—to do with me."

"It's a phase," Noelle said.

"An ugly one," Angie said, picking up her wine glass for a gulp. "Honestly, I've barely gotten a text from her since I've been here."

Eve shook her head. "That hurts."

"She's sixteen, Ange," Noelle reminded her. "Give it time. She's going to need you at some point, and when she does, you'll be there for her. And that will go a really, really long way."

Angie looked at her sister, stunned by the insight of that advice. "I hope you're right, sister. And I just hope that when she needs me, it's not serious. Like, I'm not ready to be a grandmother."

Eve gasped. "You don't think..." Then she made a face. "Sorry, I sound stupid and naïve."

"You're not, but you can imagine how I worry. I mean, my marriage is not exactly a great role model for her. If you heard some of the things Craig says to me, your hair would curl."

"Gosh, that's awful, Ange," Noelle said. "Have you considered counseling?"

"He'd never go."

"How about an honest, heartfelt conversation?" Eve asked. "Or a vacation, just the two of you?"

"I guess, but, let's be honest—he'd never go." She swallowed, gathering herself to confess the truth that she hadn't quite had the guts to say. "Being here, away from him, is the happiest I've been in months. Doesn't that bode pretty terribly for my marriage?"

As her sisters sighed with sadness and pity, Angie leaned back onto the throw pillows and shook her head, hating how genuine that statement was.

She inhaled sharply, letting the words flow from her heart out to the people she knew she could trust the most. "From the moment I arrived at the cabin, I felt a weight lift off of my shoulders. I've felt a sense of excitement and belonging and home in a way I'd forgotten was possible."

They nodded, understanding and just letting her talk because, whoa, she needed to.

"And, of course I miss Brooke, but I miss who she used to be. I miss when we were buds and we'd go shopping and get In-N-Out burgers together. It's hard to miss her when I don't even know who she is."

"Sweetie." Eve shook her head. "Noelle is right. She will outgrow this stage. Or something will happen and no one but her mother will be able to help her."

"It's hard to imagine that right now."

Noelle angled her head, taking a sip of her wine. "What about Craig?" she asked delicately. "Do you miss him?"

Angie ran her fingers through her hair, realizing the question gave her a burn in the pit of her stomach.

When she thought about Craig, her heart got heavy and sad, and her mind filled with worries and doubts. In the recent times she'd tried to connect with him, he'd only ever been distant and cold. Mild at best.

It was hard to miss someone who'd already cut her out months, even years, ago.

"I don't know. Again, I miss who he used to be."

"Why don't you call him?" Eve suggested. "Why don't you just get on the phone with him and tell him how worried you are about your marriage right now? Men can be, well, dense. He might have no idea you're this unhappy."

Angie considered that, and the suggestion had some merit. Craig did live in his own little world and maybe he'd be sad to find out she had these feelings.

"I don't know," she said. "He hates when I bother him at work and it's afternoon there. The heart of his busy day."

"Angel Chambers Messina." Eve looked at her sternly. "You are his wife. Call him. Or I really do fear your marriage is going to slip away from you."

Angie bit her lip, drawing in a shaky breath, hearing the sense of their words. "You're right. Maybe I'll give him a call after dinner."

"Not maybe. You have to tell him how you're feeling," Eve insisted. "Be honest and real. All might not be lost."

"She's right." Noelle nodded. "You've got to try."

"Okay." Angie chewed her lip, knowing she shouldn't

be nervous to talk to her own husband, for crying out loud.

It was just that they'd grown so distant, and she couldn't remember the last time they'd had a deep, intimate discussion or talked at length about their feelings for each other.

He'd probably think she was losing it entirely. And, at times, she felt like she was.

"After dinner," she said. "When he gets home from work tonight. It's three hours earlier there." And, she thought, a million miles away.

WITH A TUMMY full of Sonny's homemade chicken and dumplings and a heart full of her sisters' encouragement and support, Angie was ready to pick up the phone.

And this wasn't going to be a "checking in" call. This was not going to be a standard, four minutes of, "How are you? How's Brooke? How's work? Goodbye."

No, not tonight. Tonight, Angie was going to dig deep and channel the feelings she'd had on her wedding day, the magnetic attraction and unwavering adoration for Craig Messina that floated her down the aisle.

They spoke vows. They made promises. She could still save everything.

She shut the door of her room, knowing Noelle would give her privacy for this. Perched on the edge of the bed, she ran her hands along the patchwork of the quilt that was spread across it, gathering courage as she touched the stitching in the shape of a maple leaf.

On a deep breath and a quick prayer, she called him.

After several rings, it went to voicemail. Angie decided that what she had to say was certainly not to be left in a voicemail box.

That was okay. She'd call his office and get through the old-fashioned way when Shayna, his admin who always worked late, answered.

After a couple of rings, she heard the bright and familiar voice of a woman who'd worked for Craig since he'd started at Atlas. "Craig Messina's office. How can I help you?"

"Hi, Shayna, it's Angie. Could you put me through to Craig, please? He's not picking up his cell."

"Oh, hi, Mrs. Messina. He's still in Sacramento for the government relations meeting," she said with an air that assumed Angie knew exactly where her husband was. "He mentioned that he might need the hotel for two nights, so you could call and see if he checked out. He might just be driving home and there's lousy service up there. Or he's coming back in the morning."

"Oh, sure, I can do that." He'd be furious that she tracked him down, but, heck. She was his wife, right? She'd bet every other spouse at the meeting knew what hotel their loved one was in.

"He's at the Kimpton Sawyer in downtown," Shayna said with her clipped efficiency. "They might not put you through with just his name, but he wanted a very specific suite, so just tell them to ring nine-one-nine. I know that's where he stayed last night and maybe he's still there. Hang on, I have the number here. Ready?"

She wrote down the phone number and thanked Shayna, sitting still on the bed for a minute after hanging up. Okay, this wasn't just calling his cell to chat. This was...stalking him. At least, that's how he'd see it. He never told her where he was staying.

But why would he stay in Sacramento on a Friday night when the meetings he'd gone up for were over? She didn't know, but somehow felt that was all the more reason to call.

With fingers that were quivering a slight bit more now, Angie dialed the number.

"Kimpton Sawyer Hotel, this is Charles. How can I help you?"

"Hi, Charles. Can you ring room 919 for me?"

"I'm sorry, our hotel policy is to only ring rooms by guest names and numbers. Can you tell me who you're calling and I can confirm the room?"

"Craig Messina in suite 919," she said, waiting for a few seconds and the click of a keyboard.

"Yes, ma'am. Hold on, please, and I'll put you through."

A couple more rings and Angie's heart was racing. After what felt like forever, the line clicked.

"Hello?" a woman answered.

Angie felt her heart fall into her stomach and the earth shake beneath her.

Okay, okay, she thought to herself. Maybe he put her through to the wrong room. Maybe it was a mistake.

Maybe Craig checked out and the guy at the front desk didn't know it.

Or maybe her husband was in a hotel room with a woman.

"Hello," Angie croaked, her nervous voice shaking. "I'm trying to reach Craig Messina."

For a moment, she heard nothing. With each passing second, the black pit in Angie's stomach grew bigger and darker and—

"Can I tell him who's calling?" she asked, sounding...tense.

Angie opened her mouth to say her name, but something stopped her. Something...dark and suspicious and really, really scared.

"My name is Ms...." She looked down at the quilt, panic rising. "Maples," she said quickly. "Craig's assistant gave me the number so I could speak to him about the..." What had he told her before she left? "The new ad agency briefing in New York. It's urgent I speak to him."

Liar, liar. He was going to be furious if she—

"Okay, well, sorry," the woman said on a laugh. "He's in the shower right now but if it's urgent, hang on."

The *shower?* "Oh, yes," she ground out. "It's urgent."

"Hey, babe!" the woman called, barely muffling the phone. "You have a call from the new ad agency and they said it's urgent." She gave a throaty laugh. "Nice suds, big guy. Should I take a message?"

The words muffled through the phone or maybe that was the deafening sound of Angie's pulse pounding so hard it shook her whole body. Her throat felt like it was closing and her head felt like it was spinning.

This simply couldn't be real. It couldn't be happening.

But she finally knew the truth and all she could do with it was...hang up.

With her finger pressed on the End button, she crumpled to the floor next to the bed and sobbed.

Chapter Seventeen

Noelle

How DID it happen that she was the happiest of the triplets? Noelle, who'd arrived in Asheville with a bit of a chip on her shoulder and no interest in cabin or country, was the one most excited about the tree lighting in Pack Square. Not counting Sawyer, of course, who was as amped up as usual.

But as the three Chambers sisters and Eve's boys climbed out of the van after finding a choice parking spot, it was eminently clear that on a scale from one to ten, Noelle was an eight tonight. She wore jeans, boots, a puffy jacket and a smile that was hard to hide because she was meeting Jace and Cassie at the tree lighting. There was a hint of snow and anticipation in the air, after having spent several days and evenings with him and each date was just a tiny bit better than the one before.

So, yeah, she might even be a nine on that scale.

Eve barely hit five because an emergency surgery had kept David in Charlotte all day with no real shot of him making it to the festivities tonight. It had her sister a little sad and grumbling that whatever David wanted to do could just be taken off the table because he was never around.

And poor, dear Angie was in the mood basement.

"I don't want to go home," Angie muttered as she slid her arm into Noelle's to navigate up a slight hill and past quaint shops toward Patton Avenue, which was already packed with tourists.

"Don't." Noelle gripped her tighter. "Stay here as planned."

Her sister shot her a look. "I have to confront him. I have to let him know that I know."

"You don't think he figured it out when shower girl told him you hung up? And then he called you and you ignored him? He knows you know."

"Whatever. I have to go back to California tomorrow and..."

"And?" Noelle pressed.

"Ask for a divorce, I guess. Demand he tell me if he's having an affair."

Noelle lifted a dubious brow. "If? She called him 'babe.'"

"Do you think it's a long-standing kind of thing or just a fling?" Angie asked.

"Does it matter?" Noelle asked. "It's cheating and that's unforgiveable."

They'd all talked it to death last night, over Irish coffee and a sea of tears. Cheating was inexcusable and Angie knew it. She'd still been weepy when they finally went to bed, and when Noelle had awakened at three, she heard her sister sniffling.

When Noelle went to comfort her, Angie said that it had hit her that she had to go back to California immediately, and not only did that mean giving up Christmas at the cabin, it meant walking away from her volunteer job at Biltmore House. That realization brought on even more tears.

"This way!" James called, leading the way like a tour guide walking them around a corner and toward a darling chocolate shop, threading through groups of tourists like a man on a mission. "Uncle Sonny and Aunt Elizabeth are way up front holding spaces for us."

"Is he always this competent?" Noelle asked Eve, who hung back to join in on their conversation.

Eve smiled. "He always steps up when David's not around. Which"—she made a face—"seems to be more often than not."

"Hey." Angie reached out to her. "At least he's performing brain surgery and saving lives and not showering with...nice suds."

Eve bit her lip. "Sorry, honey."

"What does that even mean?" Angie asked. "Where did he have those suds?"

"I don't want to know," Noelle said. "But I firmly disagree with your decision to go home tomorrow."

"Me, too!" Eve exclaimed. "Just call him, fight it out, and stay here. The last thing you should do is go running back to him."

"I'm not running back to him," she insisted. "But what about poor Brooke? He's just ignored her all this time."

"Isn't she with her boyfriend's family in Tahoe?" Eve asked.

"I think so, but I don't even know." Angie dropped her head back with a grunt. "I'm the worst mother and wife ever, and I can't hide my head in the sand or snow or Biltmore House any longer. I love you guys and I love it here, but I'm going home to pick up the pieces of my shattered life and try to figure it out. It's the worst, but I have to."

The three of them paused at the corner when the light changed, letting the boys go ahead.

"I hate that you're leaving," Eve said. "But I'm starting to believe that if I ever want to see my husband this holiday, I might have to take the boys and go home, too."

Noelle groaned. "Great. Then I'm the only one here?"

"Well, you won't be alone," Angie said, leaning into her. "'Cause that cute guy right there? He ain't lettin' you out of his sight, darlin'.""

She laughed at the faux Southern drawl and followed Angie's gaze across the street to where the boys were gathered with Sonny, Aunt Elizabeth, and...oh, *man*. Did Jace have to look that good?

He stood taller than anyone else around, in a jean jacket over a navy sweater. Faded jeans, boots, and a little girl in a bright pink puffer completed the look of perfection.

From across the street, he managed to snag her gaze,

holding it with a smile in his eyes and a tilt of his head that beckoned her closer.

Cassie spun as if she sensed where her father's attention was directed, waving madly. "Miss Noelle! Come and be with us!"

"Miss Noelle, huh?" Angie whispered. "How long until that's, 'Mommy, come and be with us.'"

Noelle's eyes flashed at her sister. "Are you serious?"

"I'm not in a joking mood."

"Angie! I barely know the guy, and we live a thousand miles apart, and—"

"And he's a widower on a ranch and has a kid and goats and whatever. Yeah, yeah, yeah, I've heard all your silly arguments, sweetie." At Noelle's look, Angie shrugged. "Hey, just 'cause my marriage is a disaster with a capital D doesn't mean something better might not be in store for you."

"Angie, you can't..." Eyes wide, she turned to Eve for help, but that sister looked downright overjoyed at the idea.

"Some things are meant to be," she said softly, brushing back a lock of her pale blond hair. "You and Jace were always...connected."

"Twenty-five years ago," she countered. "Since then, we've built different lives and priorities. I have a job in New York that I love and an apartment and I just met him as an adult a stinking week ago."

"Methinks she doth protest too much," Angie stage-whispered to Eve.

"Yeah, 'cause not one reason why they can't fall madly in love has passed her lips."

"Madly in..." Noelle glanced across the street to where the group was talking and laughing, and somehow he was involved in that conversation but slyly looking at her like he couldn't wait for her to join them.

Every cell in her body melted. Was that...love?

Please don't be love. Please don't be love. Please, God, don't—

"Come on, the light's changed." Angie gave her a nudge. "And someone's waiting for you."

"My aunt," she fired back, striding across the street and straight into Aunt Elizabeth's arms.

"There are my dearest darlings!" She hugged them one after another and they all exchanged greetings.

Cassie snagged Noelle's hand and tugged her closer. "Sprinkles misses you," she said. "She couldn't give me a drop of milk she was so sad."

Noelle fought a laugh at Little Miss Serious. "Maybe I can come over tomorrow and help again."

"Please?" She snuggled closer. "I really like you."

"Cass." Jace came up behind them, surely hearing that much of the conversation. "Give the woman some breathing room."

"She can breathe," Cassie replied. "Right? Are you breathing, Miss Noelle?"

Glancing over her shoulder, she caught the humor and warmth in Jace's eyes, and something else. Something indefinable and wonderful and thrilling.

"Barely," she admitted on a laugh.

He took her other side so she was flanked by Flemings and did not hate it one bit.

Cassie chattered on about the tree lighting, and the only person who listened was Bradley, who seemed interested in the process. As they walked to the seats that Sonny and Elizabeth had saved near the front of the gathering, Jace's fingers brushed hers once, then twice, and the third time, he let their hands join.

"You look beautiful." He gave her hand a squeeze. "If I didn't know better, I'd swear a big-city girl is having a heck of a good time at a small-town tree lighting."

"I mean, it's not Rockefeller Center, but..." She looked up and held his smiling gaze with one of her own. "The people are nice."

"Well, choose wisely who you stand next to because this lighting comes with a special tradition."

She frowned. "It can't be that steeped in tradition, since I don't remember this happening when we were kids. It's new, right?"

"Yes, but there's a tradition," he insisted.

"Which is?"

"When everything goes very dark, right before the lights all come on, you have to kiss the person you're next to."

She felt her jaw loosen as a soft laugh escaped.

"Not kidding."

"Well, that's, uh, quite a tradition. I'll choose wisely."

He leaned into her, his lips brushing the hair over her ear. "I hope you'll choose me."

Her heart did a really stupid but undeniable flip as

they reached the spot where Sonny's daughters, Hannah and Caroline, and some others were waiting.

Jace introduced her to Keith Kelly, Hannah's boyfriend, a bearded redhead with a big laugh and a hearty handshake. Caroline's husband, Nate, and her little boy, Joshua, were there, too, along with some friends from Sonny's church and a few neighbors.

Booths were set up along the street selling hot chocolate and warm roasted nuts, giving the whole place a magical scent of the holiday. Around a giant Christmas tree, carolers dressed like they'd stepped out of the pages of a Dickens novel sang a harmonious rendition of *God Rest Ye Merry Gentlemen* while a group of "elves" worked through the crowd handing out candy canes and good cheer.

As Jace chatted to Nate and Caroline, Sonny and Elizabeth took a bunch of the kids to get hot chocolate, and Hannah and Keith walked off toward another group. That left Noelle between Angie and Eve, both of whom looked like none of that good cheer had reached their hearts.

"I hate that you two look so unhappy," Noelle said, reaching for their hands to join them.

"I'm sorry," Eve said. "I just can't. I can't do it."

"Do what? Be here without David?" Angie asked.

"Have another baby."

The other two stared at her with matching slackened jaws.

"David wants to and...I don't hate the idea," she whispered. "I know it's wild—"

"That'd be one thing to call it," Angie said.

"Insane would be another," Noelle cracked. "Also kind of late."

"I don't know that," Eve replied. "I mean, women have babies at forty all the time. It might be harder to conceive and carry, but..." She sighed noisily. "Now that he's planted the idea, I can't stop thinking about it. But not only do I worry about the physicality of it, but David's never around! I can't have an infant with a husband who works as much as he does, so I'm sad to say, it's not happening."

Angie blew out a breath. "I can see the appeal for you, Eve, but I can also see a hundred reasons to say no."

Eve nodded. "I think we're going to head back to Charlotte, too."

"Well, heck," Noelle muttered. "If you're both gone, why would I stay?"

They shot her a *get real* look and mouthed the word, "Jace."

"But David's missing the entire holiday season with his sons and that's not fair," Eve continued. "Asking him to drive back and forth from Charlotte—"

"I thought he was taking the rest of the month off," Angie said.

"I did, too, but I don't trust that any more than...than you trust your husband." At their reactions, she held up a hand. "Obviously, not for the same reasons. But he keeps telling me he's going to be here, then—"

"It's almost time, folks!" a man's voice boomed

through a PA system. "Gather 'round and get your cameras because we are about to light up Asheville!"

A noisy cheer rose from a crowd of several hundred.

"Hold tight to that special someone because first we go dark, and then we go light!"

"And that's when you kiss," Jace whispered from behind Noelle, wrapping his arms around her waist. The unexpected contact shocked her and sent a million chills up her spine.

She turned to look up at him, breathless again. "You made that up."

"Maybe I did, maybe I didn't. But I can tell you this—if you don't kiss someone, Santa is going to skip your house."

"Oooh. Big risk to take." She nestled into his arms, loving the feel of his body behind her. "Where's Cassie?"

"With the kids." He jutted his chin toward the small group that included her three nephews, Joshua, and a few others, all of them gathered as close to the giant tree as they could get. "Which means a tree-lighting kiss is definitely possible."

Just as she turned again, realizing how close their lips were, the phone in her pocket vibrated.

"Wow, I have an effect on you," he teased, making her step away with a laugh. "Plus, anyone you need to talk to is right here on this block."

"True, but some habits die hard." She glanced at the screen, which showed a text from...her boss. "Really, Lucinda? Now?" She tapped it for a quick read.

Lucinda Butler: *No one can cover the Harrington*

auction on Monday. You have to be here. I'll expect you tomorrow to prep the team.

Instantly, the breath went out of her, but for a whole different reason. No, this couldn't be happening.

"Everything okay?" Jace asked.

"Yeah. No. I don't know." She closed her eyes for a second and considered all the ways to respond, and most of them would cost her the best job in the world.

"Do you need to make a call?" Even in the noise from the crowd, she could hear the tenderness in his voice, which touched her.

Was it the best job in the world? It didn't feel like that at the moment.

"I'll just...reply."

She put her thumbs on the keyboard and tried not to think too hard.

Really tough for me to leave this month. Let me search for backup tomorrow.

She hit Send and stuffed the phone back in her pocket. *Please, please, Lucinda. Give me a break.*

"Is everybody ready?" the announcer asked again, giving the crowd a good ten seconds to holler their response.

Her phone buzzed again, making her let out a soft grunt.

"Work?" Jace guessed, looking down at her like there wasn't a crowd around them, or even family. His gaze was intense, direct, and caring.

She nodded and pulled the phone out again, hoping against hope that Lucinda would just let her off this hook.

She blinked at the screen. No such luck.

Lucinda Butler: *There is no one else. I've talked to everyone. You need to come back, Noelle, or you won't have the Harrington account anymore. Sorry, but we don't do month-long vacations at this company. See you tomorrow at five for the auction run-through.*

"Oh." It came out as a whimper of pure agony. Did she really just threaten—

"Here we go!" At the very moment the announcer called out to the crowd, everything went dark. The streetlights, the decorative lights, even the stores must have been in on it.

The crowd oohed and ahhed in the dark, the only lights a few phones held in the air.

From behind her, Jace tightened his grip, pulling her into his chest, dropping the softest kiss on her hair like a little preview of what was to come. Goosebumps exploded with a shiver of anticipation.

"You're here!"

At the sound of Eve's exclamation, Noelle started to turn but suddenly, the world went bright. Like every star in the sky lit up and the massive tree exploded to white life, bathing all of them in blinding light.

Everywhere, people gasped and clapped and hooted, but no one...kissed.

Until she felt Jace's fingers on her chin, guiding her face toward his, inching closer to let their lips touch for the first time in twenty-five years.

As her eyes closed and her whole body melted, the world around her faded back to black. All she could feel was this man, this dear friend from long ago, who gave her hope and happiness and everything she'd searched for but couldn't seem to find.

When she opened her eyes and looked into his, she could still hear Angie's voice from almost two weeks ago.

There's more to life than money.

And she just might be looking at it.

Her phone vibrated again, but she ignored it, kissing him again and making the only decision she could.

She would not be on that plane tomorrow...or anytime until this magical Christmas was over.

Chapter Eighteen

Eve

"I can't believe it!" Eve clung to David's shoulders, blinded by the tree lights and the look of pure love in his eyes. "How did you find us?"

"I've been texting Sonny for the past hour or so."

"You have?" She drew back. "He never mentioned that."

"I think he wanted it to be a happy surprise. Are you?"

"Surprised or happy?" She trilled a laugh. "I'm both."

"Good." He glanced past her to the gang of kids in the front.

"They don't even know you're here yet," she said, taking a step in that direction, but he held her firmly in place.

"They will soon enough." He pulled her into him and kissed her again. "Have you been thinking?"

She knew exactly what he meant. "Now? You want to talk about it now?"

"I just want to know if you've been thinking about it,"

he said, searching her face with nothing but hope in his expression.

"Of course I have. And up until about fifteen seconds ago, my answer was flat-out no."

He sighed and eased her into an understanding embrace. "I get that, Evie. I do. But I have some professional choices to make—hard ones—and I'm willing to consider how our life would be if I made those choices if you're willing to seriously think about having another child."

For a long moment, she just looked at him, and all the doubts and concerns that had plagued her just seemed to fly away. "It's crazy, but part of me is aching to say yes," she said softly. "I love being a mom more than anything. I adore it. I even liked being pregnant. I just..."

"Can't do it without a rock-solid husband," he finished for her. "Well, let's start with this. I am not leaving this mountain town until January third, with you and the kids. I'm not on call, not doing emergency surgeries, and not even talking to a patient until then. Every one of mine has been handed off to another surgeon."

Her heart soared at the words.

"Let's take the next few weeks to think hard about it," he said. "We can talk about every aspect, good, bad, and...sleepless."

"I never minded the sleepless nights," she said. "It's the pressure of doing it all so perfectly."

He lifted a brow, silent, but she got the message.

"I could learn to give up some control," she conceded.

"And I could learn to give up some patients to other fine doctors," he replied.

She took a deep breath. "You're here and we'll talk and then—"

"Dad!" The chorus of young voices interrupted them, and suddenly they were surrounded by the happy faces of their sons.

David greeted them each individually, with hugs and high-fives and an off-the-ground scoop of Sawyer, who squealed with unabashed delight.

"You made it!" Sonny came over, holding Elizabeth's hand, and the others joined, everyone laughing and sharing the moment.

Eve turned to find her sisters, her gaze first landing on Noelle, who stood holding Cassie in her arms, tapping her nose as they laughed. Jace had one protective arm draped around Noelle, his whole face looking like a man who'd just won the lottery.

"Look at those two," Elizabeth whispered in Eve's ear. "Or three, I should say. They were meant to be together."

Eve turned to her. "Did you...think about that when you called us here?"

"That romance? Not in particular, but God is the King of Surprises, isn't he?"

"He must be," Eve agreed on a laugh. "But it seems your boyfriend is vying for that title, too. Did you know he was texting David for the past hour, getting him here in time for the lighting?"

She drew back, and it was clear she did not know that. "I wonder why he didn't tell me that?"

"I guess with so much going on..."

Elizabeth turned to Sonny, stepping closer. "You managed to get David all the way here and never mentioned it to me."

"I can do a few things without you knowing."

"Oh, can you now?"

"Like this." He put two fingers in his mouth and let out a loud, shrill whistle, bringing the group—and lots of other people around them—to complete silence. "Can I have all the Chamberses, Whitakers, McPhersons, and anyone else related to me by DNA or love gather up here, 'round the tree, please?"

"You gonna climb it, Uncle Sonny?" Sawyer asked. "'Cause I would."

They laughed at that, chattering among themselves and following Sonny's instructions. A small group moved as close to the massive tree as they could get, all bathed in the brightness of a thousand sparkling white lights and silver ornaments that reflected the world around them.

At Sonny's efficient instructions, they formed a semi-circle, a little bit of confusion and a lot of questions as they did, including several from Aunt Elizabeth, who didn't like to not be in the know.

"Sonny? What's going on?" she asked.

"I just have a li'l somethin' to say to the folks here." He gestured them a few steps closer, and looked from one person to the next.

Holding David's hand, Eve let her gaze travel over

the group, which included familiar faces and new ones, but each and every one mattered very much to Sonny. And it was clear from the smile on his face and the spark in his eyes that he knew that as he waited for every sound to stop.

"My friends and my family, new and old," he said to the hushed group. "We stand here together, in the light of this tree, celebrating the upcoming birth of our Savior. But we're also celebrating being a family..."

Eve and David shared a long and meaningful glance.

"And being in love."

She looked over to Noelle and saw a soft flush deepen in her sister's cheeks. Right behind her, Angie closed her eyes as though the words hit her in a very different way.

"And to that end," Sonny said, "I have something to ask this lady right here." He turned to Elizabeth, whose eyes suddenly widened.

As he dropped to one knee, everyone gasped and let out a collective, "Oh!" that sounded as beautiful as a song.

"Elizabeth Maria Whitaker, you are the light of my life and the love of my heart. Ever since the day I found you, I believed that God had a greater plan for me, one that..." He shook his head. "One that I never saw comin'."

A soft laugh rolled through the group, but not from Aunt Elizabeth. She stood with both hands covering her mouth, looking down at him, tears ready to spill.

"I do not want to live one more year on this Earth without you by my side day and night, sharing my home, my life, my family, and my name." He reached into his pocket and pulled out a small black box and held it toward her as he opened the lid. "Would you do me the honor of marrying me and making me the happiest man alive?"

For what felt like three long heartbeats, no one spoke as Elizabeth shuddered with an unsteady breath.

"Yes!" she exclaimed. "Oh, yes, I will!"

The rest was drowned out by a noisy cheer and wild applause and pure joy as he put a ring on her finger and stood and kissed her right off the ground.

Sonny let out a hoot and spun her around, then held her still. "New Year's Eve?" he asked as they all quieted.

"Yes, of course!" she agreed. "That'll give me a whole year to—"

"Bitsy, darlin', were you not listening to my speech? I said I don't want to spend another year without you. I say *this* New Year's Eve. In just a few weeks!"

Elizabeth's jaw nearly hit the ground along with everyone else's, but then she threw up her hands in surrender. "New Year's Eve it is! Girls, you better be ready to help me plan a wedding!"

"But we have Christmas first," Sawyer called out, on his tippy-toes for attention.

"You're right, son," Sonny said, reaching down to pick him up. "Christmas and Santa is first. I just got my gift a little early. What do you want?"

"To catch a bear!"

Everyone laughed and cheered and stayed about as happy as they could be, walking through town to their cars, planning what was turning out to be a very eventful holiday.

THE BOYS DROVE HOME with David, leaving Eve alone with Angie and Noelle on the way from town back to the cabin.

"You can't leave now," Noelle said to Angie, leaning forward from the backseat to say that for what had to be the tenth time since they got in the van. "We have to plan a wedding!"

"*You* have to plan a wedding," Angie said. "I have to confront my husband and reclaim my daughter. And Eve"—Angie jabbed her arm—"has to make another baby."

"We're talking about it, not making it," she reminded them. "It's a huge decision, which we will make here, *while* we plan a wedding."

"Hey, I put my job on the line and texted my boss that under no circumstances could I come back before January," Noelle said.

Angie turned and shot her a look. "Not just because of the wedding," she said. "I saw you reading your phone before the lighting thing, and I saw you...make the decision. And by that I mean making out like you were fifteen down by the creek."

Eve chuckled at that, but Noelle just sighed and leaned back. "You're right about the timing of my decision," she said. "But not the making-out like we were fifteen part. The man has learned how to kiss in twenty-five years. All the more reason for you to stick around and tease the life out of me."

"Don't think I don't want to," Angie said glumly. "I haven't even had the nerve to call Marjorie and break the news, but I will tomorrow. Dang. I finally find something that thrills me and Craig ruins it."

They were quiet for a moment, as the high of the last hour wore off and they turned onto Creekside Road.

"It's so dark," Eve mused, hitting her brights. "Shouldn't we see the house lights by now?"

"I bet we forgot to turn them on before we left," Angie said. "Sonny wasn't there and he's always the one that works those switches."

"Well, we'll beat the boys home," Eve said. "David's car was parked so far away, I think we have them by a good twenty minutes. But it's so dark we could run into a bear."

"And Sawyer would never forgive us," Noelle joked, but Angie just shifted in her seat with the saddest sigh.

"At this point, I don't even know if I'll be back for that wedding," she said softly.

"You have to," Noelle said.

"We'll make it work for you," Eve promised as she turned the last corner, squinting into the moonless night to make sure she saw the mailbox and then turned onto the long driveway. "You know that."

"I don't know anything," Angie murmured, dropping

her head into her hands. "I don't know who my husband is sleeping with or where my daughter is."

As the bright headlights spilled on the complete blackness of the cabin and the front of the property, Eve gasped at the sight of someone sitting on the steps, putting a hand up to shield their eyes from the light.

Was that... Could that be...

"Angie?" she said softly, not wanting to freak her out. "I think I know where your daughter is."

Angie dropped her hand and looked at Eve. "What do you mean?"

"Isn't that her?"

Angie let out a shriek as she stared into the light beams. "Brooke! What is she—" She didn't finish, flipping off her seatbelt as Eve stopped the van, knowing Angie was about to bolt.

"What's going on?" Noelle asked, practically climbing into the front when Angie took off, leaving the door open. "How did she get here and why?"

"I'm sure Angie left her the address in case of an emergency, which this might very well be. Let's give them a minute."

With the lights on the pair, they could see Brooke and Angie face to face, both talking, hands moving, and suddenly throwing their arms around each other. Their shoulders shook with tears.

"Come on," Noelle urged. "I want to know."

They both climbed out, but Eve left the van lights on to guide them over the gravel and snow.

As they reached them, Brooke and Angie separated, both faces tearstained.

"What happened?" Eve asked, bracing for the explanation. "Are you okay, Brooke?"

She just managed to swallow and nod. "I'm okay," she said gruffly, swiping back a mess of dark hair. "But I need my mom. I need to be here with her. I need my mom." She sobbed the last word and folded back into Angie's arms.

Angie looked over her head to her sisters. "You were right," she whispered. "She needs me. And I guess I'm not going anywhere for a while."

Eve and Noelle stretched their arms around the other two, huddling together with more questions than answers, and the bone-deep knowledge that whatever was ahead for this holiday, they could face it together.

DON'T MISS *Book Two of the Carolina Christmas trilogy!*
The Asheville Christmas Gift *rolls us right back into the holiday with family, friends, and festive holiday drama!*

The Carolina Christmas Trilogy

The Asheville Christmas Cabin – book 1
The Asheville Christmas Gift – book 2
The Asheville Christmas Wedding – book 3

Looking for more books by these authors? Visit our websites for information and links to all of our sunny beach reads, all set in Florida and available in digital, audio, paperback, and in Kindle Unlimited - www. ceceliascott.com or www.hopeholloway.com.

About the Authors

Hope Holloway is the author of charming, heartwarming women's fiction featuring unforgettable families and friends, and the emotional challenges they conquer. After more than twenty years in marketing, she launched a new career as an author of beach reads and feel-good fiction. A mother of two adult children, Hope and her husband of thirty years live in Florida. She spends her non-writing time walking the beach with her two rescue dogs, who beg her to include animals in every book.

Cecelia Scott is an author of light, bright women's fiction that explores family dynamics, heartfelt romance, and the emotional challenges that women face at all ages and stages of life. Her debut series, *Sweeney House*, is set on the shores of Cocoa Beach, where she lived for more than twenty years. Her books capture the salt, sand, and spectacular skies of the area and reflect her firm belief that life deserves a happy ending, with enough drama and surprises to keep it interesting. Cece currently resides in north Florida with her husband and beloved kitty.

Made in the USA
Middletown, DE
06 November 2023

42049232R00163